MW01074796

MY DARK AMAZON

THE CHILDREN OF THE GODS BOOK 6.5

I T LUCAS

FOLLOW I. T. LUCAS ON AMAZON

THE CHILDREN OF THE GODS

FOR EXCLUSIVE PEEKS

JOIN *THE CHILDREN OF THE GODS* VIP CLUB

AND GAIN ACCESS TO THE **VIP** PORTAL AT ITLUCAS.COM

CLICK HERE TO JOIN

INCLUDED IN YOUR FREE MEMBERSHIP:

- **FREE** NARRATION OF GODDESS'S CHOICE—BOOK 1 IN THE CHILDREN OF THE GODS ORIGINS SERIES.
- PREVIEW CHAPTERS.
- AND OTHER EXCLUSIVE CONTENT OFFERED ONLY TO MY **VIPS**.

MY DARK AMAZON
A Kri & Michael Novella

Copyright © 2016 by I. T. Lucas
All rights reserved.
No part of this book may be reproduced in any form or by any electronic or
mechanical means, including information storage and retrieval systems,
without written permission from the author, except for the use of brief
quotations in a book review.

NOTE FROM THE AUTHOR:
My Dark Amazon is a work of fiction!
Names, characters, places and incidents are products of the author's
imagination or are used fictitiously and are not to be construed as real. Any
similarity to actual persons, organizations and/or events is purely
coincidental.

CHAPTER 1: KRI

"*A*re you okay?" Kri asked.

Michael cast her a sidelong glance. "Why do you ask?"

She shrugged.

As he steered her green Hummer through the busy Los Angeles streets, it appeared that Michael wasn't in a talkative mood. Kri didn't mind. The silence suited her; she was comfortable with it. Except, this wasn't like him. Normally, her boyfriend wasn't the silent brooding type. Was he anxious about meeting his old college buddies after not seeing them for so long?

Or was he nervous about introducing them. Kri wasn't exactly typical girlfriend material, unless one had a taste for the Amazon-warrior-woman type.

Kri smiled.

Luckily for her, Michael did.

It must be about explaining his long absence.

For months, his friends hadn't heard a word from him. Fates only knew what they had imagined had happened to him. The last time they had seen Michael, the three had been on their way back to their dorms when they'd been attacked by Doomers.

Her fellow Guardians had gotten there just in time to intercept.

Regrettably, though, she hadn't been invited to participate in the Doomer butt kicking. As a female Guardian—the first and for now the only female Guardian—she was relegated to internal policing duties. Kian would never allow her on missions involving Doomers, afraid of her falling to the enemy. It irked that he underestimated her skills, but she understood his concern. Captive of Doomers, the fate of an immortal female would be worse than death.

All she would have to look forward to, would be a never-ending cycle of brutal rapes.

Of course, Michael's friends had no recollection of the attack. Yamanu had taken care of that, thralling them to believe that Michael had left because of a family emergency.

A shiver ran down Kri's spine as she imagined what would have happened to Michael if the Guardians hadn't gotten there in time. He and his buddies were big guys, strong from years of football practice, but as humans they hadn't had a chance against the immortals. Even now, with the superior strength he'd gained following his transition, Michael still lacked the combat training to overcome one Doomer, let alone three.

Besides, his venom glands were still inactive. It would be several more months before he could do any damage with his new baby fangs, as Kri liked to call them, annoying the shit out of him. Michael was so proud of his fangs. Except, without the venom, they were not only useless as a weapon, but lacked the ability to elongate.

Bummer.

Poor guy, he couldn't wait to sink these babies into her neck, and frankly she couldn't wait either. After more than two decades of hooking up with measly humans, she was more than ready for immortal sex. After his transition, Michael had gained the stamina and staying power, but she couldn't wait for him to give her a venom bite so she could finally experience its euphoric effect. Supposedly, there was nothing that could compare to the ecstasy that followed.

She sighed. "I thought you might feel anxious."

He lifted a brow as he glanced her way. "About the fake ID?"

"No. With this new one you have nothing to worry about." Even though Michael would be turning twenty-one in exactly twelve days, and would have no more use for it, William had made him a professional quality counterfeit ID that would pass any scrutiny. "I was talking about seeing your friends after all this time."

Michael shrugged. "Why should I be nervous? We talked on the phone and they bought the story I told them." He turned into the club's parking lot.

"Let's go over it again, so I don't mess it up." Given the line of cars in front of her Hummer, they had a few minutes before the attendant could get to them.

"It's the same story I told my parents when I accepted Kian's offer to stay at the keep. It wasn't as if I could have told them the truth even if I was allowed to." He chuckled. "I can just imagine it. Hey, Mom and Dad, just wanted to let you know that I'm taking a break from college and staying with a bunch of immortals. They claim I might be a dormant carrier of their immortal genes, and one of them is going to beat the shit out of me and bite me with his fangs because that's the only way to activate them." He snorted. "They would have suspected drugs and got on the first available flight to drag me to rehab."

"Yeah, you're right. So what story did you end up telling them?"

"That I've been recruited into a special training program by a secret organization that is unofficially affiliated with the government. If I pass the finals, the organization will finance the rest of my studies at their own facilities. If I don't, they'll reimburse me for the semester I've missed. I'm not allowed to talk about it, so this is all I can tell them."

"And you told your friends that you met me at the program, right?"

"Yes. So you can claim the same bullshit; that you're not allowed to tell them anything about yourself. Yada, yada, yada."

"I like it. It's a simple story with not too many details to remember. But what if they ask how this secret organization approached us?"

He smirked. "Same answer, baby. We are not allowed to disclose any details."

"Sounds good to me." Kri reached into the glove compartment and pulled out the bottle of cologne she'd bought for him. "Here, take this and spray it all over yourself."

"Why? Do I stink?" He lifted his arm and sniffed at his armpit. "Nah, still fresh. I showered and used the deodorant you got me."

Early on in their relationship, this had been a point of contention. Michael had thought nothing of skipping a shower, and he'd believed that deodorant and cologne should be used only when going out on dates.

In some ways, he was still so immature. What did she expect, though? After all, he was not even twenty-one yet, and she was forty-seven. They only looked the same age. Never mind that as an immortal, she was considered the equivalent of a human teenager.

"This is to mask your scent, you big oaf. So spray it liber-ally. I'd rather you stink of too much cologne than for your own natural scent to be easily detectable by other immortal males."

Michael glanced at her with an amused smirk. "My baby is afraid of Doomers?"

She crossed her arms over her chest and pushed her chin out. "We are unarmed, and I'd rather spend a nice evening getting to know your friends than worry about fucking Doomers."

"Fine." He shook the bottle a few times before spraying the thing all over his clothes and his hair. "Is this good enough?"

"That's plenty." She coughed, her eyes tearing up from the stuff. Damn, it was hard to breathe in the enclosed interior of the car, and she rushed to open the window and stick her head out.

Michael shook his head. "From what I understand, it's not about the smell. I think it's the pheromones that alert immortal males to each other."

She pulled her head back inside and fanned herself. "This cologne is made with them, and supposedly in high concentration, so it might do the trick. It's better than nothing, right?"

With a whole platoon of Doomers scoping clubs and sniffing for immortal males, she didn't want to take a chance. A team of them might happen to be at the one they were going to.

Michael shrugged. "I suppose."

As the car in front of them was driven away by one of the guys manning the club's valet station, Michael let the Hummer roll forward.

Forestalling the attendant, Kri pushed the door open and jumped down. "Thanks," she said.

The guy took one look at her and stepped back, giving her plenty of room.

He wasn't the first dude to react to her this way. But that was fine. She liked the effect she had on people. Her thick-soled boots added an extra inch to her height, rounding it up to a solid six feet. But it wasn't only the height. Her shoulders were wider than those of most guys, and so were her biceps.

With a wink, she tugged on her leather jacket's lapels and closed it, hiding the girly blouse she was wearing under it. Ugh, she hated the feel of the silky material against her skin, it was odd, almost like it was wet.

Why, oh why had she let Amanda convince her to wear it?

Kri missed the familiar comfort of a T-shirt, which was what she normally wore to clubs and elsewhere. Rhinestones for the clubs, plain for every day. But Amanda had argued that a nice blouse would make her look less intimidating to Michael's friends.

She had even tried to get Kri into a skirt.

Yeah, right, as if ever.

As far as clothes, the blouse had been her only concession. The jeans and the combat boots and the jacket stayed. The one other compromise had been letting her hair out of the tight braid. Frankly though, she had done it for Michael and not as a gesture to appease Amanda. He loved to see her long hair hanging in loose waves down her back.

Michael wrapped his arm around her waist, and she tucked her hand inside his back pocket. He was only a couple of inches taller than her. But it was more than enough. Her guy was built like the linebacker he was. Next to him, she didn't look so big.

Ugh, she still remembered the endless teasing she'd suffered in the human high school. It had been such an effort not to beat the shit out of those guys. But she couldn't show how strong she was. Even considering her size. So she'd gritted her teeth and waited until graduation, knowing she'd never have to see those people again.

"Damn, I haven't hung out with humans since high school."

"Really? How about college?"

"I didn't go," Kri mumbled under her breath.

Fuck, until now, she'd somehow managed to avoid telling him, letting him assume that she'd attended.

Michael stopped in his tracks and turned to her. "All this time, you were giving me grief about not wanting to go back to school, while you never went? Don't you think it's hypocritical of you?"

"I just want what's best for you, that's all. I had my reasons for not going, and this is not the time or the place to talk about it. You are still so young, Michael, you should have fun before you settle for the first job prospect that comes your way. Why miss on the college experience? Maybe you'll find something you like better than becoming a Guardian? You can always join the force later. It's not like you don't have all the time in the world to do both."

His lips pressed into a tight line, and for a long moment, he regarded her with a hard look that belied his youth. "I'll make you a deal. I'll go back to school if you come with me."

Say what? Where did that come from?

With a smile, Michael touched a finger to the crease that had formed between her eyes. "Don't look at me with this frown. Everything you just said to me applies to you as well. You too have all the time in the world, so why give up on college? Right?"

He'd got her good, and there was nothing she could say to dispute his logic. Except—

"We are short on Guardians. This is not a good time for me to take a break. It would be selfish."

Michael wrapped his arm around her waist and pulled her tight against his side as he led her to the front door of the club. "The same holds true for me. They need me."

She rolled her eyes at him as he opened the door for her. "But you're not a Guardian yet."

He cocked a brow. "As you're well aware, I'm their best recruit."

"Ugh, you are so frustrating." It would take him decades of training until he reached the level of a Guardian. Taking a few years off to finish college would not make a dent on this long timeline, especially if he continued training during school.

"Let's call a truce for now. Here is Zack." He waved at a bulky guy with a buzz cut.

The one sitting next to him was probably Eddie, and the third one was a girl with too much makeup who was giving Kri the evil eye.

She elbowed Michael. "Who's the bimbo?"

He groaned. "Gina. God, I hope she is with Eddie."

"An ex-girlfriend?" Kri fisted her hands, then forced them to relax by her sides.

"Just someone I've flirted with a couple of times."

"That's why she's looking at me with those hateful eyes."

He squeezed her hand. "Ignore her. She's a nobody."

As they reached the table, Michael and Zack did the whole shake, embrace, and clap thing, then it was repeated with Eddie. Gina got up and sauntered up to Michael, giving him the once over as if Kri wasn't standing right next to him.

Skinny, short, with long black hair—not her natural color —Gina was wearing a clingy black dress that had ridden up her thighs as she'd gotten up. But she made no move to try and tug it down.

"Michael, I've missed you. Where have you been?" She threw her arms around his neck, pulling him down to kiss his cheek.

Eddie watched the display with a scowl, shifting from

foot to foot as his girlfriend, or date, or whatever she was to him was throwing herself at another guy.

Poor schmuck.

Michael was trying to peel Gina's hands away from his neck, but she was holding on like a little monkey.

Time to end this.

With a deadly looking smile, Kri tapped the girl's shoulder.

Still plastered to Michael, Gina turned her head around, the sweet smile she had for him replaced by an expression that belonged on a demon. "What?"

Kri glanced down at Gina's behind. "Your ass is showing." She leaned into Gina's ear. "Thought I'd save you the embarrassment, you know, one girl to another." She winked.

Gina tugged her dress down with one hand, keeping the other fastened around Michael. But Michael had had it with her, and pulled her hand away not too gently, then pushed her toward Eddie. She stumbled, but the guy caught her.

Michael wrapped his arm around Kri's shoulders. "Guys, I want you to meet my girlfriend, Kri."

She shook hands with everybody, including Gina.

"You're really tall." Despite the five-inch platform shoes she was wearing, Gina had to crank her neck to look up at Kri.

Kri bent at the waist, lowering her face to Gina's level. "Or maybe you are really short. It all depends on your perspective." She winked and slid into the booth to sit next to Michael.

"Why don't you take off your jacket, baby?" Michael said as he took his off.

Hell, why not. Give little Gina some competition for the slutty look. Kri unsnapped her leather jacket and shrugged it off, then quickly readjusted the two overlapping halves of her silk wrap blouse. Immediately, like four heat-seeking missiles, Eddie and Zack's eyes homed on her cleavage.

Kri rolled her eyes. She wondered if it was only the effect of hers, or did every set of double Ds reduce men to drooling idiots. And if so, then she needed to think of a way to use her big boobs against her enemies. A distraction could provide just the edge she needed when facing a larger and stronger opponent.

"Eyes up here, boys." She motioned with her fingers.

The embarrassed stammering was interrupted by the waitress who arrived to take their order.

"What can I get you?" she asked, her eyes zeroing in on Michael as a light blush crept up her cheeks.

Odd, to say the least.

Michael was handsome, but so were his friends, not that they could hold a candle to her man, but still, they were fine male specimens. So what was with these females and their crazy focus on her guy?

Of course!

Kri slapped her forehead. The fucking pheromones—they were actually working—not as concealment from other immortal males, but as an attractant to females.

Damn.

CHAPTER 2: MICHAEL

"*How* long have you guys been dating?" Michael croaked as Gina's hand landed on his thigh. Unfortunately, squished as he was between Kri and the handsy Gina, he couldn't scoot away. The booth they were sitting in was designed to accommodate four average-sized adults; not three massive football players, a large female Guardian, and one skinny girl whose wandering hand was inching up his thigh. Michael would have swatted it away, but he didn't want to cause a scene.

"A couple of months." Eddie wrapped his arm around Gina's slim shoulders. The guy had been lusting after the cheerleader for ages. Seeing her flirting with another guy must sting like hell.

Gina was probably drunk, or maybe even high, and Eddie was a saint for putting up with her. Or maybe he was just desperate. Be that as it may, as long as Eddie could pretend that he didn't know what was going on under the table, he wouldn't be forced to dump Gina's butt.

Kri, however, was a different story.

As much as Michael felt bad for Eddie, the guy was the

least of his concerns. Kri wasn't a hothead, but she was possessive, and God only knew what she would do if she noticed.

Still, maybe she had. It would explain her uncharacteristic quiet. Kri was acting strange, fidgety, preoccupied. It wasn't like his normally outspoken and often rowdy girlfriend to barely string two sentences together throughout the evening.

He found it unlikely that Gina's flirting was the cause.

Maybe Kri was worried.

After all, Doomers were scouting clubs, searching for immortal males, and Michael had his doubts about the effectiveness of the cologne he'd doused himself with before coming in. The scent couldn't be strong enough to mask his natural body odor against their superior sense of smell.

Come to think of it, Kri was emitting a very distinct scent of her own, and it dawned on him that she was actually in greater danger than he was. Under normal circumstances, an immortal female emitted no unique scent and was therefore undetectable to other immortals. Which was probably the main reason none of the clan females had ever fallen into Doomer hands. Except Amanda, but that was a different story. Dalhu had recognized her face from a picture. When turned on, however, the smell of an immortal female's arousal was very different to that of a human's, and easily detectable to any male immortal. This was the only time she was exposed and vulnerable to Doomers.

Michael leaned away from Gina and got closer to Kri. "Do you want to go home? You seem antsy," he whispered in her ear.

"You think?" she hissed. "These damn pheromones are driving me and every other female in the vicinity insane."

Oh. Not cool. So it wasn't his irresistible male magnetism that was turning Gina into a lusty slut and making his girlfriend squirm in her seat.

How disappointing.

Michael nodded. "Well, we'd better head out." He motioned for Kri to get up and slid out of the booth after her. "It was great seeing you, guys, but it's getting late. Kri and I have an early morning class tomorrow." He clapped hands with Zach, then took Eddie's offered paw. "We should do it again soon."

"It was nice to meet you," Kri managed to bite out as she leveled a chilling glare at Gina, forestalling her attack on Michael.

"Let's go, baby." Michael wrapped his arm around Kri's waist and walked her out.

"I'm sorry," she said.

"About what?"

"Cutting your evening short because I was horny. I tried to ignore it, but it was impossible. My panties were soaking wet and my nipples were trying to poke holes through my bra. They still are. I didn't hear anything you guys were saying. All I could think about was jumping your bones. That cologne was a stupid idea. I didn't think it through."

Not necessarily.

The effect all that talk about wet panties and hard nipples had on Michael was just as powerful as what the pheromone-imbued cologne did to Kri. He couldn't wait to be inside her.

In fact, the fifteen minutes or so drive to their apartment in the keep was too long.

He hugged her closer, running his palm up and down her sashaying hip. "How about we find a dark place and scratch that itch? I don't think I can wait for us to get home."

She bumped her hip against his. "I like the way you think."

Outside, Michael gripped Kri's hand, pulling her with him as he headed around the back to the alley behind the club. There was a deeply recessed doorway there, leading to a storage room that would be locked tight for the night. He'd been there before, necking with a girl whose name he couldn't remember. The nook was dark and secluded. As far as he knew, no one went there during the night. In short, it was perfect for a quickie.

Except, as they rounded the corner, his enhanced hearing picked up the unmistakable sounds of slurpy kisses and hushed moans. Damn, someone was there. Apparently, his hiding place had been discovered.

Kri tugged on his hand. "Come on. Let's check that building." She pointed to the next one over.

"Okay."

Michael was grateful for Kri's long legs and purposeful gait as they passed one building after the other and still found no recessed nook they could use. Other than the club's back wall, all the others had doors that were built flush with the exterior. No recesses meant no privacy, or the illusion of it.

He stopped and pulled her back. "Let's go back to the car. We're wasting our time."

"No, look over there, that courtyard. We can hide behind those bushes." Kri sounded breathless, but he knew it wasn't due to their fast pace. She was excited. His girl liked to take risks and live dangerously. Having sex somewhere where there was a chance of them getting caught, turned her on like nothing else.

It wasn't perfect. The place was wide open to the alley. But there was a tree in the middle of the small courtyard, and it was surrounded by rose bushes. The shadow it cast on the building behind it would have to do.

For once, he had no problem accommodating Kri's exhibitionist bent. He was so desperate for her that he was willing to do it with an audience.

Almost.

Michael let her pull him to a stretch of wall that was shaded by the tree. As she shoved him against it, her mouth smashed over his and her hand cupped his shaft through his pants.

He palmed her ass, squeezing, then trailed his fingers down to the seam. Damn, she was so wet she'd soaked her jeans through.

"Oh, baby, you really need me inside you, don't you?" He licked her throat and bit down, his useless little fangs nonetheless piercing her skin. Tasting blood, he licked the wounds he'd made closed so he could bite her again, and again. Kri groaned, loving his teeth on her. Without venom, there was not much else he could do for her, but at least his saliva carried the healing agents to help Kri's immortal body close them fast, so he could bite her again. A poor substitute for what she wanted and needed, but for now it was all he had to offer.

She moaned, her hips gyrating against his crotch.

He loved her assertiveness, but he needed to be inside her, and for that they needed to switch places.

Kri didn't protest when he turned them both around, pressing her against the wall. Wrapping her arms around his neck, she was busy kissing and nipping every bit of exposed skin. "Take my pants down," she hissed into his ear and then licked the earlobe, sending shivers of pleasure down his spine.

He did as she'd asked, popping the button on her pants and pushing them down her hips, then doing the same for his and freeing his shaft. Problem was, with her pants only halfway down, she couldn't wrap her legs around him, and discarding them altogether when they were out in the open like this was too risky.

He rubbed his erection against her slickened slit. "You should start wearing skirts."

Kri harrumphed. "Not going to happen. Back off a little so I can turn around."

Facing the wall, she pressed her hands against the rough brick facade and bent a little, pushing her gorgeous ass out like an offering.

Fuck, what a sexy sight.

Just to see her like that, he would bring her to this spot again.

Bracing with one hand against the wall, Michael gripped his shaft with the other and guided it into Kri's wet heat. There was nothing he wanted more than to shove into her and start pumping, but instead he teased her entrance, coating himself with her moisture.

It still felt weird not to use a condom.

Protecting himself and his partner had been hardwired into his brain. Except Kri had pointed out that diseases were no longer a concern, and that her chances of getting pregnant were nearly nonexistent.

She pushed back, trying to get him inside her. "Don't tease me, Michael."

With a groan, he obliged her, gripping her hips and pushing into her in one strong thrust. Kri's stifled moan sounded almost like a growl, and she started moving, pushing and retreating, dictating the tempo she needed.

Fuck, he was going to spill, like right now.

"Don't hold back, baby. This is just round number one."

She was right. He could erupt inside her and still be hard, pumping her with another load within minutes, and then another, and then another. Even before his transition, his stamina had been impressive, but now he was like a tireless seed-producing machine.

Immortality was awesome, but this unexpected perk was at the top of the list.

Oh, the good life.

CHAPTER 3: KRI

*A*s the orgasm rippled through her, Kri leaned her forehead against the rough wall.

Michael was still going full force, pounding into her from behind and prolonging her pleasure. The skin on her forehead must've been scraped raw, but she didn't care, the high of endorphins was blocking the pain. Besides, she knew the abrasions would heal in no time at all. She was boneless with pleasure and keeping her head up on her neck was too much of an effort.

Michael was killing her. In the best possible way.

His rugged breathing and the swelling of his shaft prepared her for the eruption that followed, and she clenched her inner muscles around him, milking him for all he'd got. Which was plenty. Even though he was spent, Michael kept pumping a little longer before sagging against her back and enveloping her body with his larger one.

What a wild ride.

There was something about being exposed like this that thrilled her like nothing else. She'd indulged only a couple of times before, and only with Michael, but all three times the experience had been so intense that she was starting to get addicted to it. It wasn't that she was an exhibitionist—performing in front of others was not her thing—but she craved the excitement of almost getting caught.

It appeared that she was going to get more than she bargained for.

With Michael breathing heavily in her ear, she almost missed the faint sound of conversation getting nearer.

She bucked Michael off. "Hurry, get your pants up. Someone is coming."

Now that he was paying attention, he heard it too, and she didn't need to tell him to be quick about it. They were both properly dressed by the time the voices got louder and a group of young men headed straight into the small court-yard. She flattened her back against the wall and pushed Michael to do the same next to her. Hidden in the shadows, she waited to see what they were up against before making her move.

"Hey, gimme some." One of the guys snatched a half empty bottle of some kind of alcohol from his friend.

There were eight of them, the youngest about seventeen and the oldest in his mid-twenties.

The one whose bottle had been taken didn't fight for it. He passed it on, and as he lit up a cigarette, the tiny flame cast a narrow strip of light on his face. He looked haggard, and the hand holding the cigarette, or rather the joint by the smell of it, was shaking.

Damn, a druggie.

The one with the bottle passed it to someone else and lit a joint of his own.

They were not going anywhere.

The good news was that they were only a bunch of puny humans, nothing she couldn't handle. The bad news was that there were eight of them, which made them dangerous, not because they outnumbered Michael and her, but because being in a pack made them stupid. Things they would've never dared do on their own, in a group might seem like a great opportunity to impress their friends.

There was another problem, though. Two were wearing jackets, which on a warm evening like this could mean only one thing. They were carrying. Question was, what?

Knives or guns?

Not that it mattered. Neither could do real damage to an immortal unless the punks knew what they were doing, which they obviously had no way of knowing. No one in their right, or even impaired mind would think to cut out their victim's heart to make sure they were dead.

Except the Aztecs. Those fuckers must have known something. More likely, though, they had been nothing more than bloodthirsty savages.

Whatever. Now was not the time for contemplating history.

Appraising her unimpressive adversaries, Kri knew she could dispatch the punks with ease. They posed no real threat to her. The problem was how to do it without killing any of them. Her strength and her training made her a capable killing machine, but Kri had never ended anyone's life before, human or immortal, and she wasn't about to tonight. Her first kill was reserved for a Doomer.

She put a hand on Michael's shoulder. "Let me handle this and follow my lead."

First rule of conflict, avoid it if you can; second rule, try to disarm a combative situation before it explodes: third rule, if you have to fight, make sure you win.

The best thing would have been to sneak out without being noticed, but the courtyard was small and enclosed on three sides, with the gang blocking the exit.

So the first one was out.

She would have to try influence. This whole episode could be avoided if the punks let her sway their tiny minds. Stepping out of the cover of shadows, she took Michael's hand and walked toward the mouth of the courtyard. As no one looked their way, she hoped they'd get lucky and manage to slink away.

"Lookie here," the one with the bottle slurred. "What have we got? A couple of pussies?"

Damn.

"Evening, gentlemen," she said in a confident tone imbued with influence. The subliminal message was simple—ignore the uninteresting strangers.

It worked on the drunk one with the bottle, but the one with the shaking hand was apparently too high and antsy to accept her mental suggestion.

"Not so fast, bitch. We're not done talking to you."

Beside her, Michael tensed and tried to pull his hand out of her grip. She held on. There was still a chance to disarm the situation without anyone getting hurt.

Kri kept walking, practically dragging Michael behind her, when she heard the unmistakable sound of a gun being cocked.

"Bitch, I said I was not done talking to you. Come back here and bring your pussy of a boyfriend with you."

Okay. With one and two exhausted, it was time for rule number three.

CHAPTER 4: MICHAEL

One of the bastards pulled a gun.

Michael's first instinct was to shove Kri behind him and shield her with his body. Except, he was too slow. While his mind was processing the situation and sending messages to his legs and arms to move, Kri dropped his hand and flew at the group of lowlifes.

The bastards never knew what hit them.

With a roundhouse kick, Kri disarmed the guy holding the gun, probably breaking his arm because he dropped to the ground and was howling in pain.

"What the fuck?" A buddy of his tried to swing at her, only to get dispatched with one powerful punch to the face. His broken nose was bleeding like a geyser.

Kri grabbed the heads of the third and the fourth, knocking them against each other, then dropped the two unconscious dirtbags where they stood.

It had taken her no more than a couple of seconds to take down four guys, during which Michael just stood there, paralyzed, watching her in awe.

"Who's next?" she paused to taunt.

He knew what she was doing.

Kri was giving them a chance to scram, but the idiots were too stupid to realize that they had already lost.

When another one pulled out a switchblade and flicked it open, Michael got moving, launching himself at the guy.

"Fuck!' He heard Kri curse. "Now, why did you have to do this?"

What the hell? Did she expect him to stand on the sidelines and watch while she took care of business?

He grabbed the guy by the wrist and twisted it. There was a pop and a snap and the switchblade cluttered to the ground. The scumbag fell to his knees, clutching his broken wrist.

Satisfied with how quickly he'd disarmed the guy, Michael turned to the next assailant, but he was a split second too late.

First, there was a burning pain, and then the asshole with the butcher knife got really close and pulled the thing up, slicing Michael open. A moment of confusion followed, and as something warm and sticky saturated his shirt, Michael's foggy brain interpreted the sensation as warm piss.

Had the guy pissed on him?

Dimly, he was aware that piss wasn't supposed to be sticky.

Then he passed out.

The blackout must've lasted no longer than a few seconds, because when Michael opened his eyes, he saw Kri deliver an uppercut into the guy's gut, sending him flying a few feet back. She followed, delivering a kick that must've pulverized the guy's ribs, either making sure that he was out cold or avenging Michael. In any case, the motherfucker had it coming.

It got quiet then, and all Michael could hear were Kri's panting breaths and his own wheezing ones.

She dropped to her knees beside him. "Let me see." She pushed his hand aside and grimaced. "That's a nasty one. I bet it hurts like a son of a bitch."

Yeah, it did. But not as much as his pride.

Kri put his hand back where it was. "Hold it there. The bleeding will stop in a minute or two. You're lucky to be an immortal. A wound like that could've been fatal for a human. He gutted you good."

Michael groaned. This was a serious injury. The guy must've been either fucking strong or pumped up on drugs to plunge the knife so deep and then drag it up Michael's middle, creating a long cut that had no doubt injured internal organs.

As he tried to sit up, he had to hold on to Kri so as not to fall back. The loss of blood was making him dizzy, and he knew he needed her help to get up.

As if he wasn't feeling like a complete failure already.

It had been humbling, and quite discouraging, to realize how inadequate he was in a real fight. Evidently, the opinion he had about himself had been grossly overinflated. Compared to Kri's, his skills were pitiful. She'd taken out seven guys while he'd barely managed one, and what's worse, he had gotten himself nearly eviscerated in the process. Failing so miserably against untrained humans meant that he'd been deluding himself when he'd thought he could ever take on a Doomer—an immortal with superior strength and training.

Damn, there was no way he'd be able to get to the car, and asking Kri to carry him was just not going to happen.

It was painful to talk, but he had no choice in the matter. "I don't think I can make it back to the parking lot. Could you go get the Hummer and drive over here?" Michael hated how weak he'd sounded.

"I'm not leaving you here alone and defenseless, not unless I first finish these guys off. Except, even though they are too stupid to live, I don't want to have it on my conscience."

She wrapped her arms around his torso and lifted him to a standing position.

Michael winced, stifling a groan as the pain became overwhelming. Kri did not move, letting him catch his breath while supporting his weight. Damn, the woman was strong. Stronger than he'd given her credit for.

"You'll have to lean on me and try to walk. If your injury wasn't in your stomach, I would have carried you fireman style, but you are too tall and heavy for me to carry you in my arms."

Michael nodded, letting Kri reposition him so he was leaning against her side, and she was propping him up at the hip. He was going to walk to that fucking car if it fucking killed him, and he was going to grit his teeth and pretend he wasn't about to faint from the pain. Because if she changed her mind and decided to carry him princess style, he would rather drop dead.

"Okay, big guy. We are going to do it slow and easy. I need you to hold on only until we reach the front of the building. It'll be relatively safe for you to wait on the street until I bring the Hummer around. It's well illuminated, not like that dark alley, so even if one of the scumbags regains consciousness and goes looking for you, he won't dare do anything in plain sight of cars driving by…"

As Kri kept talking, he knew she was doing it to distract him from the pain and was grateful for it. His vision swam in and out and he almost blacked out a couple more times, but he made it to the front of the building without collapsing, which was a huge accomplishment considering how excruciating the effort had been.

She left him slumped against a window display that provided a narrow ledge he could sit on, and sprinted toward the parking lot of the club. He watched her long legs eat the distance—powerful and graceful at the same time.

God, he loved this woman.

Michael closed his eyes, letting his head drop against the cool glass behind him. He'd never told Kri how he felt about her. Not because he was unsure, and not because he was scared that she might not respond in kind. He knew Kri loved him.

In her own way.

Funny, how in real years he was less than half her age, and yet he felt as if it was the other way around. In her head, Kri thought of herself as a teenager, and any mention of long-term commitment scared the shit out of her. If he told her he loved her, she might bolt.

Which would be awkward since they lived together.

Not to mention devastating.

In his heart, Michael knew that he wanted to spend eternity with Kri, and if she would've had him, he would've proposed on the spot. But that was before he'd been proven useless. No wonder she'd been pressuring him to go to college. Kri must've known he wasn't really Guardian material. She and the other Guardians must've been humoring him all this time.

Had they been laughing behind his back? Joking about the kid who thought he could be a Guardian?

He had nothing to offer Kri.

He'd better pretend that he wasn't serious about their relationship either. It wouldn't be a big stretch. No one expected a guy his age to make grand pronouncements of everlasting love and propose marriage.

Was he weird to want it so desperately?

Naive?

Maybe. But maybe not. He wasn't too young to realize that there was no other woman like Kri. She was unique, and he found her perfect. So why wait or look elsewhere when he was so damn lucky to already have his one and only true love?

CHAPTER 5: KRI

*S*hifting in his seat, Michael groaned. "I'm sorry."

Kri cast him a worried glance. His wound should have closed already. Instead, the blood oozing from it was pooling between his legs.

He was such a tough guy. Gritting his teeth and enduring the pain without passing out, which was astounding considering the amount he'd lost and was still losing. True, the bleeding was no longer as copious as it had been right after he'd been stabbed, but it was still worrisome.

"What are you sorry for?"

"The seat. I'm bleeding all over it."

Silly guy. As if it was of any importance.

"Don't worry about it. It's just a car, and the seats are leather. I can clean it up no problem. What I'm worried about, though, is that your wound is not closing. You should've stopped bleeding already. When we get home, I'm taking you straight to Bridget. In fact, I'm going to call her and let her know we're coming. That way we won't have to wait for her. She can meet us down at her clinic."

Michael shook his head. "No, I'll be fine. It will close any moment now."

"I want Bridget to take a look. Maybe she needs to stitch it, or maybe there is damage to your internal organs that she needs to do something about. I'm not a doctor, but this is not a scratch you can slap a band-aid on."

Shaking his head again, he gritted, "You don't get it. I don't want anyone to know."

Aha, so that was his problem. But why? Kri furrowed her brows. "There is nothing to be embarrassed about. Even Guardians get injured from time to time and seek medical treatment. I don't understand why you feel like you need to hide it."

He didn't answer her, but the mutinous expression on his face said it all.

Fates, why were men so stubborn and stupid?

Not wanting to upset him further, Kri pulled out her phone and texted with her left hand so Michael wouldn't see what she was doing. Texting while driving was dangerous, not to mention stupid, and most of the time she refrained from doing it, but this was an emergency.

Lucky for her, Kri was ambidextrous—a pretty useful trait, and not only for texting with her left hand tucked against the driver-side door. She could deliver a knockout punch with either fist, and handle a weapon equally well with her left as with her right. Not that she was a great fan of weapons. Mixed martial arts was more her thing—she liked it up close and personal.

The wide boulevards of downtown Los Angeles were practically deserted at this time of night, and with Michael in no shape for a chitchat, there was nothing to distract her from noticing the occasional homeless vagabond. Watching the dirty bundles, sleeping on a bench or tucked inside a doorway, Kri felt the familiar pang of regret and a smidgen of guilt.

Something should be done about it. But what?

She was a Guardian and a good fighter, but that was about it. Since she was a little girl, this was all Kri ever wanted to be. She wasn't a social reformer, and she had no grand ideas for how to solve this problem. Donating a few dollars here and there was not going to help. It really sucked to see a wrong and not be able to do shit about it.

Nearing the keep, she looked up at the imposing high rise. The place screamed of wealth and opulence—a sharp contrast to the squalor dotting the rich landscape of some of the city's most expensive accommodations.

Driving down the keep's underground parking, Kri reached the lowest level and waited for the heavy garage door to slide open before easing into her spot in the clan's secure parking area. Good old Dr. Bridget was waiting for them, leaning against the wall with her medical bag dangling from the fingers of her hand.

Michael growled. "I told you not to call her."

"I didn't. I texted her. Don't worry, she's not going to tell anyone. She is a doctor. Don't they swear some oath not to reveal patients' information? The hypocritical oath?" She was mispronouncing it on purpose, trying to get a smile out of him. But Michael was either too pissed at her or in too much pain.

As Kri killed the engine, Bridget came over and opened Michael's door. "Let's see what we got here." She lifted his hand off his wound and nodded approvingly. "You were smart to pull up your shirt before the blood crusted over and glued it to your skin. The bleeding has stopped, but I need to see what's going on inside. Can you walk? I didn't bring the gurney."

"It's okay, I don't need it." He made a move to get out and winced.

"Hold on, let me help you." Kri came over to his side and offered her arm. "Slow and easy. Put your hands on my shoulders and just slide out." A stomach wound hurt like a bitch, not that she'd experienced it herself, but she'd heard the guys talking about it.

Leaning on her only slightly, Michael grunted and pushed himself out. She didn't urge him to move, knowing that he needed a moment to collect himself as he breathed through the pain.

A few seconds later he lifted his head. "Dr. Bridget, is there a chance you can do your thing at our place? I don't want anyone to know."

Bridget chuckled. "Sorry, buddy, but I need to check your insides with the ultrasound machine. Unless you prefer I just cut you open again to take a look?" She cocked one red brow.

"Fuck!" Michael let his head drop on his neck.

Kri patted his shoulder. "I have an idea. How about we go home first and clean you up, put a new shirt on, and then go down to Bridget's clinic. That way, if anyone does see you there, they won't know why you're visiting her."

Michael cast Bridget a hopeful glance.

"Fine. A few more minutes will not make much of a difference. But don't take too long, okay?"

"I'll have him there in ten minutes tops."

Bridget popped her bag open and pulled out a white packet. "For the pain." She handed it to Kri.

"Thank you." Kri stuffed it in her pocket.

"It's not so bad. I don't need painkillers," Michael said as soon as they were alone in the elevator.

Idiot.

As if she couldn't see him fisting the hand he wasn't

holding over his stomach, protecting it even though it was no longer necessary. The wound had stopped bleeding.

Kri rolled her eyes. "Yes, you do, and you're going to take them. Suffering needlessly is not a sign of bravery."

His eyes, usually so warm and affectionate, were stone-cold as he pinned her with a hard stare. "Stop babying me, Kri. You're my girlfriend, not my mother."

Shit.

He looked and sounded pissed.

It must've been the pain talking.

Michael had never spoken to her like that before. In fact, she loved that he was a positive kind of guy, not grumpy or demanding like Kian.

Fates, she couldn't believe she'd ever had a forbidden crush on her uncle. Now that she had Michael, Kri realized that he was a much better fit for her, and it had nothing to do with the taboo against mating within the clan. Kian, or any other man with his sort of personality, would have been the worst match for her. Easygoing, friendly, and upbeat was what she needed.

Michael was so young, though. Had she really been babying him?

Kri cringed. Yeah, she probably had.

First, it had been about the deodorant. But that was still in the realm of what a girlfriend would insist on. After all, a woman had to have a say in how her guy smelled. And anyway, what was the point of showering each morning but then forgoing the antiperspirant and stinking a couple of hours later? Right?

Then there was all that talk about going back to college. But again, a caring person wanted what was best for their partner, and the same was true about not letting him suffer needlessly.

None of these issues were the exclusive domain of mothers.

Besides, according to Syssi, and even Amanda—who no one could accuse of motherly inclinations—men needed their women to save them from making dumb macho decisions.

Except, Michael wasn't stupid, or too full of himself not to realize that she only wanted what was best for him.

Damn, this was probably about their age difference.

As it turned out, Kri was only two years younger than Michael's mother. Apparently, even though the subject had never come up, it bothered him. It didn't matter that Kri didn't look a day over twenty, or that for an immortal she was considered very young.

Evidently, somewhere in the back of Michael's mind this was an issue.

CHAPTER 6: MICHAEL

"*I*'m going to the gym." Michael wiped his mouth with a paper towel and took his plate to the sink, rinsed it out, and put it in the dishwasher. The least he could do in this relationship was not to become a burden. Kri shouldn't have been washing his dishes, or doing his laundry. In fact, he was furious at himself for letting her do all those things for him before.

So yeah, he'd been in charge of cleaning the bathroom and vacuuming, but considering she worked full time and he didn't, he should've been doing all of the household chores, not just a portion of them.

"Are you sure you're up to it?"

"Yeah, I am. I'll see you later." He waved before walking out, closing the door quickly to avoid seeing the hurt look on Kri's pretty face.

He hadn't kissed her goodbye.

This was the third morning since the incident, and Michael was going crazy from doing nothing but watching the dumb tube all day.

Enough was enough.

He had to get out of the apartment or he was bound to start smashing things. Things that didn't belong to him…

It had taken him two long days before he had felt like his old self again. Well, almost. According to Dr. Bridget, his internal organs had healed perfectly and no medical intervention had been needed.

Physically, he was back to normal; emotionally, he was a mess.

Problem was, his efforts to hide it and put up a front weren't fooling Kri for a moment. She kept nagging him to talk to her, tell her what was wrong, but he couldn't. How could he admit to her that his confidence had gone down the shitter? Or that all his plans for the future had puffed out of existence like the illusion they'd been?

Watching Kri in action had been a nasty wake-up call. It had become poignantly apparent to him that he didn't have what it took to become a Guardian. He would never be as good.

Well, perhaps never was too strong of a word. If he trained like a motherfucker, day and night for years, he might pass the entry exam.

Damn, he'd been deluding himself that he could join the force in a few months, when in fact he would be lucky if he could accomplish it in decades.

The only upside, as far as he was concerned, was that over those long years he wouldn't have to worry about his body aging. Physiologically, he would remain as young and as healthy as he was now.

Except, there was the issue of earning an income while training. Kian had authorized a pretty generous monthly allowance for him, and living with Kri he had no big expenses, but that had been okay as a temporary arrangement, only until he entered the force and started earning a Guardian's salary. Hell, even a minimum wage as a Guardian's apprentice would have been great. Receiving an allowance for doing absolutely nothing was demeaning.

It would have been different if he'd been born into the clan. Every member was getting a share of the clan's profits. Except, even this seemed like mooching to him.

He wanted to contribute.

The elevator descended, and as Michael watched the floor numbers scroll down an idea popped into his head. Maybe he should listen to Kri and go back to college, but switch majors from economics to accounting.

Damn, he couldn't believe he was actually considering it. But as his father had said, accounting may not be the most glamorous or interesting of professions, but there was always work for accountants.

It wasn't difficult, and Michael was good with numbers. He even had some work experience.

His father had insisted on him spending the summers working in his office and had taught him the basics. It had been boring, no doubt about it, but it hadn't been all bad.

Michael would never admit it to his dad, for fear that his old man would never let it go, but there was something strangely satisfying about closing a file with the numbers neatly balanced and everything in order.

In its core, accounting was a lot like arithmetic—it wasn't open to interpretation. Things either balanced or they did not. It wasn't a matter of opinion. Which was kind of cool.

Hell, what was he doing? Channeling his inner nerd?

Glancing at the mirror, Michael couldn't help a snort. He was a tall guy, with shoulders that were wide and heavily muscled from years of playing football. He would look funny sitting behind a desk and crunching numbers.

Like his dad.

His old man had been the star of his high school football team, but he hadn't been good enough to pursue it any further. He was a damn good accountant though, and his uninspiring, cluttered office had provided well for his family.

Still did.

The elevator doors swooshed open and Michael exited, heading for one of the new training rooms instead of the main gym.

Brundar should be teaching a class in one of those.

As it turned out, Brundar had been right about the importance of endless repetitions, learning the defense moves and training the body until muscle memory set in and the responses became automatic instead of thought through. Michael had learned it the hard way. If he'd followed Brundar's advice and kept training with those four basic moves, he would've been able to block that knife attack.

He was going to ask the guy to resume his training. There was no one better than Brundar, and God knew Michael needed the best help he could get.

Problem was, Brundar had been busy lately, but Michael was willing to beg if necessary.

He wasn't going to tell the guy why he was so desperate to train under him. Brundar was the silent brooding type who hardly ever said anything at all, but in this case Michael had no doubt he would hear the dreaded I-told-you-so.

More than the training, though, Michael needed reassurance. He wanted Brundar to tell him that he could make it one day, even if that day was in the distant future. Or conversely, tell him to forget it and set his eyes on something more achievable.

Like accounting.

The other Guardians were too nice. Michael didn't trust them to tell him the truth. Brundar, on the other hand, didn't give a shit about people's feelings. Michael knew that the guy wouldn't lie to him just to spare him. If Brundar didn't believe in him, he would tell it to his face without sugar-coating it.

There were no windows in the doors to peek through, and Michael had to open each one briefly before closing it with as little noise as he could and continue to the next one, finding Brundar in the fourth classroom he tried. Then he had to wait another ten minutes out in the corridor until the class was over.

As they left the room, people gave him curious looks. Few of the immortals living outside the keep knew of him.

He just smiled back.

Brundar was the last one out. "What can I do for you?" He didn't offer his hand. By now, Michael was used to the guy's quirks. Brundar would shake a hand if it was offered, but it was obvious he didn't like it, and he never initiated it.

"I would like to resume training with you. If you have the time."

Brundar shook his head. "Sorry, I can't. You should ask Bhathian."

Was he really so busy? Or was he just fobbing Michael off on someone else because he didn't believe he could make it?

Brundar regarded him stoically.

Damn, it was impossible to read the guy. He was either very good at hiding his emotions or didn't have any. Even Michael's telepathy was drawing a blank.

Brundar surprised him when he said, "I'm heading to the kitchen for a beer. You want to join me?"

"Yeah, sure. Thank you."

Brundar being social? Something was up.

As he followed Brundar down the corridor to the big industrial kitchen, Michael had a sinking feeling that he was about to hear a little speech about considering career prospects that didn't involve Guardianship. Usually, Michael's telepathic ability could detect intentions, or strong feelings, but Brundar was like a vault. Impenetrable.

"Take a seat." The guy motioned to one of the stools strewn around the huge center island. The thing looked to be at least twenty feet long and about four feet deep, and the surface was stainless steel.

As Brundar came back with the beers and took a seat next to him, Michael couldn't wait to open the bottle and gulp the whole thing down.

Brundar popped both caps with a flick of his thumb and handed one to Michael. "You wanna tell me what's going on?"

Fuck, it was hard to ask a question when the answer could either devastate him or make him soar to the clouds.

Be a man and just ask.

"Do you think I have what it takes to be a Guardian?"

The guy didn't hesitate for a millisecond. "Of course, I do. I wouldn't have invested my time in you if I thought you weren't worth it."

Michael fought hard not to sag in relief and to keep from grinning like a fool. "Thank you. I was having doubts."

Brundar's brow furrowed. "Why?"

Michael shrugged, trying to think of a way to say it without revealing the embarrassing details of his failure. "I watched Kri... train. She is so much better than me. I don't think I'll ever reach that level. She is the youngest of you guys, the least experienced, and a female, and still she is light years ahead of me."

That earned him the extremely rare sight of Brundar's smile. Damn, the guy was pretty when he smiled, like in almost girly pretty. Good for him that he was deadly, otherwise he might have given people the wrong impression.

"Kri is an excellent fighter, and she's been training for decades. You are a newbie. Give it time."

"How long? Like in months? Years? Decades?"

"Years. In four you'll be battle ready—as a foot soldier—not a Guardian. Give it another decade or so and you'll reach Guardian level."

Michael sighed. It was better news than he'd expected, but it still wasn't good. He would've been okay with a time horizon of four years to become a Guardian, but fourteen? Damn. He could become a medical doctor in less time. Trouble was, he wasn't that good of a student.

He had to ask. "Did it take Kri that long?"

Brundar nodded. "It did. A word of warning, kid. Don't ever let her hear you making light of her abilities because she's a female. She will have to prove you wrong and it will hurt. A lot." He ended with a wink—a shocking thing to see on Brundar's face. The guy must be in an exceptionally good mood today.

"Yeah, you're right. She is an amazing fighter." Michael raked his fingers through his short hair. "What about my training, though? Is Bhathian a good teacher? Would he take me on?"

Brundar didn't answer right away, taking his time to think while taking several swigs from his beer. "Bhathian is good. But for you, I think Arwel is better."

Arwel? The drunk? Michael couldn't remember seeing the guy ever sober. "Why Arwel?"

Brundar waved with his beer. "Because he is a telepath, like you. More powerful, and his goes both ways, not just receiving like yours, but he can teach you to use telepathy to your advantage in a fight. Anticipating your opponent's moves is half of what you're going to learn as a warrior."

Ha, interesting.

Maybe his gift could provide just the shortcut he needed to reach Guardian level sooner.

"Thank you. I'll go talk to him. You think he is free?"

One corner of Brundar's lips lifted in almost a smile. "I know he is. The challenge will be to keep him sober long enough to teach you anything."

No kidding.

CHAPTER 7: KRI

"Where are you going?" Kri asked.

Not that his gym clothes didn't make it obvious. Except, Michael had just come back less than an hour ago.

"I have another session with Arwel."

"Is this going to be the last one for today, or are you going to spend the night at his place?" She couldn't keep the sarcasm from her voice.

If Kri didn't know Arwel as well as she did, she would've suspected that there was something going on between Michael and his new instructor.

The two were spending entire days together.

"Of course not," he mumbled before slinking out the door as fast as his feet could carry him short of running.

Michael was avoiding her. And not only during the days. Every night he would come exhausted from his never-ending workouts and training sessions, grab a quick shower, and fall asleep before his head hit the pillow.

They hadn't had sex ever since the fight in the alley.

Talk about frustration.

She wasn't going to beg for it. If he didn't want her, she wasn't going to ask. Problem was, it couldn't go on like this. She needed a steady supply of sex to keep her satisfied, and without it she was becoming a danger to society.

Or as it was, to the gym equipment.

Today, she'd managed to destroy a punching bag. Which was a big deal since it had been specially designed and custom made to withstand the abuse of immortal males. The thing had survived Anandur for Fates' sake, but not her anger.

The first couple of nights she'd blamed his injury for the lack of interest. But then he'd started training again and she had to face the grim reality that he just wasn't into her. Not anymore.

She should ask Michael to leave and find somewhere else to crash. It was too painful to lie next to him in bed. Ignored. Neglected. Unloved.

Damn. Kri wiped a stray tear from her eye. She wasn't going to shed tears over the stupid schmuck. She was going to pack his things and leave them out by the door. He could pick them up and go without ever having to come in.

Damn, damn, damn. More tears came rushing down.

What a jerk.

He wouldn't talk to her either. But she had a damn good idea what it was all about. The injury, but not the one to his stomach. It was his stupid male ego that was bleeding. The idiot couldn't accept that a woman had saved his butt in a fight.

If he possessed an ounce of functioning gray matter in that thick skull of his, he would have realized that she had years of training on him. It wasn't about being less of a male, but about lack of skills.

Still, if he was stupid enough to make a big deal out of it, then he had no business being with her. She was never going to be the little woman, the fragile female who needed protection from her strong macho man. If this was what Michael needed to feel good about himself, he'd better go looking somewhere else.

Ugh. Kri hurtled her cup against the wall, watching with sick satisfaction as the coffee splattered, painting a big brown starburst. The cup clattered to the floor, by some miracle not breaking.

Fuck, still mad as hell, and now she had to repaint the damn wall. She needed to get out of the apartment, maybe go talk to someone. Except, there was no one she knew that faced a similar situation. It wasn't as if Syssi could understand her—the woman was dainty and small and feminine. Besides, Kian was too confident to ever feel threatened by his woman, even if bested by her in one thing or another.

Amanda was a better choice.

Any man would've felt threatened by a female like her, and Dalhu was in a worse situation than most. She was stunning, educated, smart, and oozed confidence. Dalhu was uneducated, penniless, and totally dependent on her. It was astounding that their relationship not only survived but seemed to thrive. Perhaps Dalhu's age had something to do with it, his maturity, or perhaps the guy was so strong, so confident, that his current circumstances didn't affect him negatively.

Kri shook her head. She should go talk to Dalhu and ask him how he managed to deal with it. Maybe he could have a word with Michael, give him some advice.

First, however, she needed to talk to Amanda. It just didn't seem right to go up to someone else's man and ask questions about such private matters. She wouldn't have liked it if another female had done that with Michael without clearing it with her first.

Pulling out her phone, she texted. *Do you have a moment? I need to talk to you.*

A few minutes later, Amanda replied. *Sure, come on up.*

One of the advantages of sharing one big building was that visiting a relative didn't require a commute. Claiming lack of privacy, some of the clan members hated it, but Kri loved it. What was the big deal about meeting someone in the elevator? It wasn't as if they all shared one big living space. They had their own individual apartments. If you didn't want to interact with anyone you didn't have to. In fact, most of the socializing happened in the gym, and even there you could choose a time of day or night when there weren't many people using it.

With the elevator ride to Amanda's penthouse taking only a few seconds, Kri was at her door a minute after receiving the invitation.

Amanda was waiting for her with the door open. "Hey, girl, come in."

"Thanks for letting me invite myself over." Kri pulled Amanda into a quick embrace.

"Any time." Amanda put her hands on Kri's shoulders and looked into her eyes. "What's going on, Kri? You look like you've been crying."

"No." Kri rubbed her eyes with her fingers. "It must be the lack of sleep." Hell would freeze over before she'd admit to Amanda that she'd been crying over a guy.

Except, the woman wasn't fooled. She took Kri's hand and led her to the sofa. "Come on, tell Mommy everything."

Kri chuckled. "I stopped telling my mom things a long time ago."

"Okay, so tell Auntie Amanda everything."

It seemed they were alone in the penthouse, but Kri asked anyway, "Is Dalhu here?"

"No, he's down in the gym with Anandur."

Oh. So maybe Dalhu was dealing with his problems the same way Michael was—spending endless hours at the gym.

"Does he do it a lot?"

"Well, yeah, every day. After all, to maintain that amazing body of his requires a lot of work." Amanda winked.

"I meant, how long? Is it a couple of hours or all day long?"

Amanda narrowed her eyes. "Why are you suddenly concerned with Dalhu's workout routine?"

Shit, she should go straight to the point instead of annoying Amanda with questions about her man. "I'm not. It's just that Michael is spending entire days training, and I have a feeling he is doing it to avoid being with me." It took tremendous effort to keep the quiver out of her voice. She was a Guardian for Fates' sake. What would Amanda think of her if she did such a girly thing?

"Why would you think that? Maybe he is just impatient to become a Guardian? You should know how much training is required."

It seemed that she would have no choice but to confide in Amanda and tell her what had happened. Except, she would be betraying Michael's trust. He'd asked her to keep it a secret.

Some dancing around the subject was needed. Hopefully, Amanda was smart enough to get the gist of it.

"I can't tell you the details, because I promised not to, so I'm going to describe a hypothetical scenario."

Amanda made a rolling motion with her hand. "Go on."

"So, let's assume that Michael and I get into a fight with a bunch of good-for-nothing humans. Naturally, I'm much better trained, and I kick ass, while Michael... doesn't. He is upset that he didn't do so good, and he gets Arwel to train him. In itself, it's not a problem, but between the hours he spends training with Arwel, lifting weights, cardio, and any other workouts he can think of, he is gone entire days. He comes home at night and is too tired to do anything other than collapse into bed and go to sleep."

Thinking, Amanda put a long-nailed finger to her lips and tapped. "You think he feels inferior? Because you're a better fighter?"

"I think he feels threatened by me. I don't know what to do, Amanda. It can't go on like this. I'm actually thinking about breaking up with him. If he can't handle who I am, then it doesn't make sense for us to stay together." Kri crossed her arms over her chest and slumped into the sofa's back pillows.

Amanda patted her knee. "You're overreacting, sweetie. Every relationship goes through some turbulence. You can't give up at the first sign of trouble. And as to the sex, maybe you should seduce him. After all, he is an immortal male—his needs are just as powerful as yours. He can't hold out for long."

Kri snorted. "It's hard to seduce a corpse. He falls asleep the moment his head touches the pillow."

"So catch him in the morning."

This was actually not a bad idea. She could put on an alarm and wake up before Michael had a chance to sneak out the way he'd been doing lately.

Kri pushed up to her feet. "You're right. I'm going to do that."

"Good luck, girl."

CHAPTER 8: KRI

*I*n her dream, Kri swatted the annoying bee that wouldn't stop buzzing around her wrist, but instead of an insect, her palm collided with a square metal object. With a jolt, she woke up and whipped her head around.

Good. Michael was still there.

She had set her watch to vibrate at four in the morning, hoping to catch Michael before he sneaked out. Mission accomplished. Well, part one was. Part two was the seduction. Easy enough. Arousing a male was simple—touch him and he'd get hard—especially a young immortal like Michael.

Kri padded to the bathroom and closed the door behind her as quietly as possible. Planning ahead, she'd washed her hair last night, cutting down her morning routine to under five minutes. A few spritzes of perfume and she was ready for action.

Except, still drowsy as hell, she craved coffee in the worst possible way.

Peeking into the bedroom, Kri made sure Michael was still snoring softly, before tiptoeing out to the kitchen to make coffee. After all, a woman needed to be awake to act all seductive. This needed to be more than a quick morning romp.

They had had many of those since they had moved in together. In fact, other than these recent, miserable days, it had been part of their routine—a quickie in the morning and a marathon session at night.

Oh, the good old days.

But they were not over yet. Not if she could help it.

Leaning against the kitchen counter, Kri sipped her first cup of the day, then plugged in the thermal carafe, grabbed another cup, and took everything to the bedroom.

She wasn't letting Michael out of there for anything other than a quick visit to the bathroom. If he wanted coffee, she would have it right there, eliminating any excuse he might come up with to get out of bed.

Carefully setting everything on her nightstand, Kri got back in bed and snuggled up behind Michael, spooning. What a shame that he'd taken to wearing boxer shorts to bed. She hated having anything between her skin and the soft bed linens, or between her and her man.

Those needed to come off.

But first, a little wake-up call.

She reached around him and slipped her hand inside his shorts. Michael groaned, his semi hard erection swelling in her gentle grip.

Was he awake?

She pressed her lips to his neck, trailing little kisses down to where it met his shoulder, then nipped the sensitive skin at the junction.

"Are you sleeping?" Kri whispered in his ear, then caught his earlobe between her teeth.

He shivered. "Not anymore."

"I've missed you." She'd meant to say something sexy, but the accusation had just bubbled up before she could stop it.

"I've missed you too." He turned around and wrapped his strong arms around her, his body stretching alongside hers.

They were a perfect fit.

She loved feeling the hard planes of his chest against her soft breasts, and the rigid length of his shaft against her belly. In the dark, in this bed, Michael felt like a man, not a boy, and she could pretend that he wasn't so damn young.

She kissed his neck again, then licked the slight mist of salty perspiration coating his skin. Fates, he tasted good. She lifted her mouth to his lips and kissed those too, loving how big and fleshy they were. With a probing lick at the seam, she asked permission to delve in, but he squeezed his lips tightly and shook his head.

"Let me brush my teeth first."

"I don't mind your morning breath."

"I also need to take a piss."

"Okay, but hurry. I've been waiting long enough already."

He closed his eyes and touched his lips to her forehead. "I know, and I'm sorry. I'm going to make it up to you. I promise."

"You'd better." She made a pouty face and slapped his shoulder playfully.

The relief was almost overwhelming, and as Michael trotted to the bathroom, Kri lifted her eyes to the ceiling and offered a prayer of thanks to the merciful Fates.

They weren't over. This had been just a bump, a hurdle, and their relationship was going to survive.

CHAPTER 9: MICHAEL

*G*od, he'd been such an idiot.

Michael banged his forehead on the vanity's mirror. When he'd woken up with Kri's incredible breasts pressed to his back, and her lips on his neck, he'd felt like a ten ton boulder had rolled off his chest.

The woman was an angel for still wanting him.

He'd been in such a bad place ever since that fight in the alley. Feelings of inadequacy, of inferiority, and of pure shame were destroying him from the inside. The only way he knew how to deal with them was to work himself to exhaustion, trying to improve.

What really hurt, though, was the realization that Kri had been indulging his fantasies. She should have told him that he wasn't good enough, that he needed years of training to reach even one tenth of her skill, if at all.

For real, though, he'd been angry, plain and simple, and in a roundabout way he'd been taking it out on Kri.

It wasn't her fault that he was ashamed, that he was feeling like less of a man ever since she'd showed him what real skills looked like. She'd been magnificent, but instead of telling her that, he'd been acting like a moron, letting his entire life revolve around his training.

A hell of a boyfriend he was.

People in a relationship were supposed to spend time with each other and make one another a priority. Instead, he'd been focusing only on himself, his feelings and his needs. On some level, he'd been aware that he was hurting Kri. She didn't understand what was going on with him. She probably thought he'd been avoiding her.

Not that she was wrong. Ever since that fight, he'd been obsessed with getting better. It was like a compulsion, and anything outside of this singular pursuit was a distraction. Including Kri.

What did it say about him?

Was it immaturity? A personality flaw?

Probably both. But he'd be damned if he let himself continue on this destructive path. He was going to make love to Kri until their bed caught fire and she begged him to stop.

Not that there was a chance in hell of that.

His woman loved sex, and lots of it. The more likely scenario was that he would drop dead from loss of bodily fluids before that.

First order of business, however, was to cease all this self-deprecating mental beating and get back in that bedroom. Dropping his boxer shorts in the dirty laundry hamper, Michael marched naked into the bedroom like a man on a mission.

Kri lay sprawled atop the bed linens, greeting him with a sexy smile and a pair of stiff nipples adorning her ample breasts.

What a sight.

The woman was a goddess.

With a leap, he closed the distance between the bathroom doorway and Kri's inviting body.

She squeaked as he got on top of her, letting her feel all of his considerable weight. There was no need to be careful with Kri. She was big and strong, and she wasn't going to get smothered by his bulk.

Perfect.

Looking at her flushed face, so beautiful, so pure, he lowered his lips to her mouth and kissed her, gently, just a feathery touch.

Even though he was burning, even though he couldn't wait to be inside her, Michael wasn't going to rush this. He wanted to do it right. Compensate for the days he'd wasted acting like an insecure jerk.

Kri deserved better.

She deserved a man who would always put her pleasure and her well-being before his own, and Michael vowed that from now on he was going to be that man.

With a ragged groan, Kri's hands shot to his neck and she forced his head down, smashing her lips over his. Hot, hungry, demanding, her tongue slid into his mouth.

God, he almost spilled from that kiss alone.

She kissed him as if she'd been starved for him, as if she had waited to do this forever. But then, she had, and it was all his fault.

His fingers digging into her hair, he cradled her head and kissed her back, pouring all of his emotions, all the things he couldn't say to her, into that one epic kiss.

Kri moaned, her hands abandoning his neck to grab his ass and hold him tight as her hips circled under him, trying to guide him inside her.

"Keep doing that, and I'm going to come," he murmured into her mouth.

She let go of his lips. "Then go for it, big boy. You've got more than one in you. Or two, or three, or four." She smirked.

True, but he'd rather be inside her each and every time.

Sliding down, he licked her nipple, his fingers rolling and tugging the other one. Then he switched, suckling and kissing the other while lightly pinching its wet twin. God, he was crazy about these breasts. He loved everything about them—the way they overflowed his large hands, the way her nipples drew tight and rigid when she was aroused, the way she responded to his fondling—her throaty moans and groans getting louder by the moment.

He wasn't done with the foreplay, though. Not yet.

Both palms plumping the heavy weight of her breasts, he shifted downward and planted a wet kiss on her lower lips.

Her thighs parting even further, she allowed him better access. Kri loved a good tonguing, and he was going to give her one to remember.

Michael was quite proud of the lover he'd become. He'd never told Kri, but his sexual experience before meeting her had been limited to only one lover. The girlfriend he'd had for a few months in his third year of college had been his first, but he hadn't been hers. Which he was thankful for. At least one of them had known what to do. Besides, she had taught him all he knew about pleasuring a woman, so he hadn't fumbled like a rookie when Kri had first taken him to her bed.

Still, that had been nothing compared to what he'd learned from Kri. She wasn't shy about what she wanted and how she wanted it, and he wasn't either.

Michael was more than happy to accommodate whatever pleased her, and that included her quirky penchant for having sex in public places. Not his thing, but if that was what turned her on, then why not.

Except, from now on, darkened alleys were out. Once had been enough.

Licking and sucking with abandon, Michael gripped Kri's

undulating hips, holding her in place as he tongue-fucked her into an orgasm. She shuddered, quaking with the after-shocks, and he licked some more, drawing out her pleasure.

"Come up here," she husked, pulling his head up from between her thighs. "I want that beautiful shaft of yours inside me."

Oh, yeah. He was all for that.

With a lurch, he got on top of her, and she gripped his length and guided it inside her. Hoisting her thighs around his hips, he retreated a little only to plow inside her with one powerful thrust.

They both groaned, clutching each other, fusing their sweat-misted bodies like they were never going to let go.

This was it.

This was his home, his life, his future. Right there with his woman, joined as one.

CHAPTER 10: KRI

"*Y*ou're in a good mood today," Anandur smirked as he helped Kri up.

They'd been sparring for a while, and she was getting tired—which was the only reason he'd succeeded in toppling her to the mat. Though bigger and stronger, Anandur wasn't as agile and nimble as Kri. As long as she moved fast enough to evade his grip, she was good. Problem was, he knew that eventually she would run out of steam and then he would get her.

Today, though, nothing could upset her. Not even losing to the big oaf. Again.

Gone was not only the sexual frustration that had been turning her into an angry harpy, but also the painful churning in her gut. Things were back to normal between Michael and her.

Almost.

He hadn't been ready to talk yet, but for now it was good enough. What was important was that they were back together.

She hadn't lost him.

"Sure I am. It took you how long to win today? Forty minutes? Forty-five? I'm getting stronger and better."

"That you are, girl. Good job." He patted her shoulder.

Kri wondered if she'd ever be on the receiving end of the bro embrace and clap. After two decades of training with them and proving her worth, the guys were still treating her like a girl.

Just to spite him, she smiled sweetly and gave him a little princess wave. Trouble was, he didn't get it, smiling back indulgently. Like he was proud of a kid or something.

Ugh, the guys had no idea how much it irked her.

It had been a good workout, though, and she was done for today. Grabbing her towel off the floor, Kri headed out and took the elevator up to her place.

Michael wasn't back yet. He was still training with Arwel in one of the converted classrooms. The guy was teaching him to use his telepathic abilities. They couldn't train in the gym proper because Michael had a hard time focusing on his opponent when there were other people around. He'd have to get over that hurdle or his telepathy wouldn't be worth shit.

After a quick shower, Kri grabbed a bite to eat, then headed out to Amanda's. They weren't done talking. Amanda had insisted that Kri must come back to report on her progress.

Trouble was, Amanda wasn't alone when Kri got there. Dalhu was sitting on a barstool and sketching a portrait.

"Darling, would you mind working in one of the spare bedrooms? Kri and I want to have a girl talk."

He grunted something, picked up his sketch and his charcoals, and headed down the hallway.

"Thank you!" Amanda called after him.

"I feel bad. He didn't look happy about being kicked out."

Amanda waved her hand dismissively. "Nonsense. He is

grumpy because the portrait isn't coming out the way he wants. Besides, I'll make it up to him later. You want a drink?"

"Sure."

"What would you like?"

"Just a beer, thank you."

Amanda pulled a bottle out of the fridge and handed it to Kri. "You need a glass?"

"No, thanks, I'm good."

She watched Amanda pour some weird, green liqueur for herself.

For some reason, Kri couldn't stand green liquids. Perhaps because they reminded her of the fresh-squeezed vegetable juices her mother used to make for her.

Blah.

Drink in hand, Amanda sauntered over to the couch and sat down, crossing her ankles. "Okay, girl, talk to me. Just from looking at you I know it went well, but I want the details."

Kri sat in the overstuffed chair facing Amanda and took a swig from her beer. "It worked like a charm. But Michael still won't talk to me about it. He's probably too embarrassed to admit it and I don't want to push him. He's having a hard time as it is."

"Yeah, men's egos are so fragile. Maybe you should compliment his size. That always puts them in a good mood."

Kri chuckled. "I did, but I really meant it."

Tapping her foot on the floor, Amanda took a sip from her disgusting drink, then put it on the coffee table and crossed her arms over her chest. "I've been thinking."

Oh boy, here it comes.

"Maybe you should soften the edges a little. You've been putting on this tough façade for so long and hanging with

57

Guardians like you were one of the guys that perhaps you've become a little too masculine."

Kri narrowed her eyes. "So what are you suggesting? That I put on a dress? Or paint my face? That's not who I am, and I'm not going to change just so Michael can feel more manly. He needs to accept me the way I am."

Amanda reached for her drink and took another sip. "I'm not talking about a personality overhaul. I'm talking about small gestures. It's not like you suddenly need to become Miss Congeniality. I'm not expecting you to start prancing around in skirts and dresses every day, but once in a while, for a special occasion or a romantic dinner at a fancy restaurant, it won't kill you to wear a dress or put on a little makeup."

Well, putting it this way, Amanda had a point. If wearing a dress once in a blue moon, on a special occasion, would improve her relationship with Michael, then she could tolerate it for one evening. Come to think of it, though, she'd gone to Syssi's wedding wearing a pantsuit, and Michael had told her that she looked beautiful. Maybe Amanda was overestimating the importance of the damn dresses because she happened to like them.

"I don't think it matters to Michael what I wear or don't wear."

"Don't be silly. Look at it this way. If you go out to a romantic dinner with the guy, and he shows up with a two-day growth, wearing torn jeans and dirty boots, you may not say anything but you are not going to be happy. But if he puts in an effort to look good for you—he shaves, puts on some cologne, a nice dress shirt, and polishes his boots—you are going to appreciate it."

"True." What could she say? The woman was right.

"So how about it? I can get you reservations at By Invitation Only, and you invite Michael to a nice dinner. Of course, I'll dress you up for it. This is not a job for amateurs."

When Kri cringed, Amanda raised her palms. "Nothing fancy. Just an elegant dress and some flat ballet shoes. I know you hate heels. And anyway, you're too tall."

"Hey, I'm only an inch taller than you, and you wear crazy heels all the time."

Amanda cocked a brow. "Do you want to wear heels?"

"No, of course not."

"So what are we arguing about?"

"You said that I'm too tall, and I pointed out that I'm not much taller than you. That's all."

The truth was that Amanda could pull off wearing insanely high heels, towering over everyone, and still have all the males drooling over her. Kri would just look like a big, square tower.

Amanda sighed. "Whatever, fine. Now let's go and try on some dresses."

Kri closed her eyes and sighed.

The things I'm willing to suffer for this guy. He'd better appreciate the hell out of me for it.

CHAPTER 11: MICHAEL

"Kri?" Michael called as he entered their apartment.

There was no answer, but he found a note on the kitchen counter.

I'm at Amanda's getting dressed. Be ready by six-thirty.

Damn, he didn't know how he felt about going to that fancy restaurant. Nervous? Excited? Frustrated?

By Invitation Only, what a pompous name.

He'd had to cut his workout routine short, so he'd have time to come home, shower, shave, and get dressed in something nice. Not that he had anything like that. The tux from Syssi and Kian's wedding wasn't an option, and other than that he only had jeans, T-shirts, and hoodies. Maybe he should follow Kri's example and borrow something.

But from whom?

Anandur was taller than him, Brundar was slimmer, Bhathian was both taller and wider. Kian's clothes would probably fit him best, but he wasn't going to ask the guy for one of his designer suits. First of all, even the simplest one in Kian's closet was probably worth a fortune, and he would be stressing throughout dinner about putting a stain on it. Second, wearing a suit to a restaurant he would feel like a fool.

Damn, she should've given him more notice. With more time, he could've run out and bought himself something decent. Like a new pair of jeans and a button-down. For shoes he could use the ones from the wedding. Black shoes were black shoes, right?

With a sigh, he picked up the receiver and punched the extension for Kian and Syssi's penthouse, hoping Syssi would answer. It would be easier to ask her for a favor. Kian was a good guy, but he was intimidating as hell.

"Kri?" Syssi answered.

"No, it's Michael."

"Oh, hi, what's up?"

"I need a favor."

"Shoot."

"Can I borrow one of Kian's dress shirts? Kri is taking me to that By Invitation Only place, and all I have are T-shirts and jeans."

He heard her chuckle. "Don't worry. I'll pick up a few and bring them down to you."

"Thank you. You're an angel. I'm going to grab a shower, but the door is open. If I'm not out yet, just come in."

"I will."

When he came out, Syssi was already in the living room with an armful of brand new dress shirts.

"Last week, Mr. Fentony delivered a bunch of new ones. Kian hasn't even looked at them yet."

"Are you sure it's okay with him?"

She nodded. "He couldn't care less. Here, choose whichever."

"Are they all the same size?"

"Yes. Same size and same cut, just the fabrics are different. I would go with the white one, always a safe bet. Or maybe the blue one to bring out your eyes. Which do you prefer?"

He took the white. "Thanks."

Syssi made a shooing motion with her hand. "Go on, try it on. I'll wait."

The shirt was a little tight across the chest, but only a little. It would work. Hell, it had to. Michael had no time to look for something else. He pulled on his best pair of jeans, the shoes from the wedding, and ran a comb through his short hair.

Not bad. He smiled at his reflection in the mirror.

Hopefully, the place had no policy against jeans. He could just imagine a snooty hostess or host turning him away. *Sorry, sir, but jeans are not allowed in here, you have to leave and come back properly dressed.* Or something like that.

When he came back to the living room. Syssi beamed like a proud mother. "Oh, Michael, you look so handsome."

He felt his cheeks heat up. "Thank you."

Syssi was only a few years older than him, and a serious hottie; he couldn't help it if her compliment made him uncomfortable.

"You sure this is the one? Do you want me to leave a couple of the others? Just in case Kri doesn't like it?"

"No. I'm sure it's fine. This shirt is really nice. Thank you."

"Okay." She scooped the small pile into her arms. "Have fun tonight."

Michael opened the door for her, and she cast him a bright smile before stepping inside the penthouse's elevator.

Syssi was such a nice person, and beautiful, but she wasn't his type.

Kri was.

Pacing around the living room, he waited for her to come

for him, wondering what was taking her so long. It's not like she ever fussed with her hair or makeup like other girls. Hell, most days she was ready before him.

A few moments later the door opened and the mystery was solved.

God, what did Amanda do to my girl?

Kri had makeup on. Not much, but even that looked weird. She was naturally beautiful, and painting over that perfection was like ruining the Mona Lisa.

And she was wearing a dress.

And earrings.

And she was clutching a handbag.

Her smile wilted as she took a gander at his expression before he had a chance to control it. "You don't like it."

Fuck.

"No, I do. It's just that I've never seen you in a dress, that's all. You look really nice."

She narrowed her eyes. "Just tell me the truth, Michael. I did this all for you." She waved a hand over her face. "I hate this stuff. It feels like I'm covered in gunk."

She had done it for him?

Wow.

Why?

He crossed the few feet between them and pulled her into a hug. "You don't have to put on anything for me." She felt stiff in his arms. "In fact, I like you best with absolutely nothing on."

That got a chuckle out of her, and she slumped into the embrace. "Should I wash it off?"

"Definitely."

"And the dress? Should I change into my regular garb?"

"Keep the dress. It shows off your magnificent legs."

"Really?" She searched his eyes.

"Really. I like the dress."

Kri pushed away from him. "Okay, wait here. I'll be right back."

It took her no more than two minutes to get rid of most of the war paint, but traces of black mascara—or perhaps it was an eyeliner, he wasn't an expert on the stuff—still framed her big blue eyes.

She rubbed at them. "I couldn't get rid of all of it because I don't have the special remover."

Michael pulled her hands away before she did more damage, and used his thumb to wipe away the new smear she'd just made. "Leave it. This little bit is actually nice, makes the blue of your eyes stand out." He used Syssi's phrase, hoping it was the right thing to say. He'd already made enough of a mess.

"You think?" She walked over to the mirror hanging by the front door.

"Yeah, you're right. This is not bad at all. And the best part is that I can hardly feel it."

Phew.

"Good. Are we good to go?" He took her hand.

"Yeah, I just need my damn purse. There are no pockets in this dress."

He reached for the small bag and handed it to her. "Let's go."

CHAPTER 12: KRI

By Invitation Only was like no other restaurant Kri had ever been to. Just to get to the place from the parking lot they had been escorted by an attendant through what looked like an enchanted garden. The guy had left them in the capable hands of the hostess, the leggy brunette who was now leading them to their reserved table. "This is even fancier than what I imagined," Kri whispered in Michael's ear.

He squeezed her hand.

Poor guy, he seemed so uncomfortable, and for a good reason. The two of them belonged in a place like that like a pair of elephants in a china shop. Even though dressed in their borrowed finery, they must've looked like the poor relatives someone invited out of charity. Not to mention that they seemed to be the youngest amongst this opulent crowd. Or at least Michael was, Kri just looked it.

Damn, everyone's eyes were following her, but it sure as hell wasn't because she was such a looker. Kri knew what they were staring at—a big woman with linebacker's shoulders and the gait of a soldier. A woman who had no business wearing a slinky, above-the-knee halter dress.

She didn't belong here, among the millionaires and their trophy dates, the movie stars and starlets, the politicians and their wives or their husbands.

Whatever.

Pushing out her chest, Kri flipped her long hair back and lifted her chin. She had a few things going for her and wasn't too modest to flaunt them. Her wavy hair was long and thick, her cleavage was impressive without the help of implants, and Michael had said that her legs looked great.

Besides, she had to remind herself that she was doing this for him.

The hostess stopped next to a small table set for two and pulled out a chair for Kri.

"Thank you." Kri smiled a big fake smile. If she was going to play a part, she'd better do it right.

"Would you care for something to drink while you're looking over tonight's selection?"

"A Perrier, for me. Michael?"

"Just water."

"Very well." The hostess inclined her head and sauntered away.

The woman was a knockout, slim with long legs that looked even longer in the spiky heels she was wearing. Those things must've been murder on her feet. Even if she weren't six feet tall, Kri would've never subjected herself to such torture.

The menus had no prices on them, but she'd known coming in that the dinner was going to cost her half a grand at least. Not a problem. She had the money. Aside from her share in the clan's profits, her Guardian pay was substantial. She had more money than she knew what to do with.

Michael frowned. "Where are the prices? How am I supposed to know what to order?"

Kri opened her purse discreetly and pulled out the small box that had been the main reason for schlepping the thing with her. It wasn't as if she had a comb or a lipstick in there, and the two plastic rectangles, her driver's license and credit card, could've fitted in Michael's pocket. She reached across the small table and took his hand. "Don't worry about it. It's my treat. Happy birthday, Michael." She lifted the wrapped box from her lap and placed it in front of him.

His surprised and delighted expression was the best thank-you he could've given her.

Michael pulled her hand to his mouth and kissed it. "I had no clue. I thought you'd forgotten."

She laughed. "Are you kidding me? Your twenty-first birthday is a big deal." Leaning towards him she whispered, "You can finally use your real driver's license to order a drink. Should we toast with a glass of champagne?"

"How about a Bud Light?"

"A Budweiser? In this place? They probably don't have something as plebeian."

"What about Snake's Venom?"

Kri snorted. "Do you want to get drunk on your birthday? Not that I mind if you do," she said with a shrug. "After all, this is your celebration. I can drive us home."

Michael squared his shoulders and shifted back in his seat. "I won't get drunk on one beer, not even Snake's Venom. I had plenty of them at Kian's bachelor's party and was perfectly fine."

Kri wanted to roll her eyes. *Here he goes again. His male ego getting hurt by nonsense.*

She patted his hand. "Whatever you want, baby. When they come to take our order, we will ask what they have. But first, open your present."

Michael lifted the box, examined it from all sides, and even gave it a little shake. "Hmm, what could it be?" he taunted.

She was so excited for him to see what she'd gotten him, and the guy was teasing her, prolonging her anticipation.

She'd spent a small fortune on this gift. He'd better like it.

"Ugh, just open it already."

With a smile, he loosened the blue silk ribbon, unwrapped the box, and popped the lid open.

Kri was practically bouncing in her chair, her eyes darting between the box and Michael's face.

"Oh, wow!" He lifted up the watch, checking it out. "This is amazing, thank you." He looked closer. "Patek Philippe? I've never heard of this brand. What is it?"

Damn. I've spent close to twenty grand on it, and he doesn't even know that this is one of the most luxurious brands in the world.

"It's a very good watch and it keeps its value. If you ever want to sell it to get a different one, it will fetch a good price. This one is their entry level watch, but that's not why I bought it. It's elegant yet young, luxurious yet understated." She smiled. "Or at least this is what the salesman claimed. Anyway, I hope you like it."

"I love it. Thank you." He put it on his wrist then pulled her hand for a kiss.

Obviously, Michael had no idea that this wasn't a mass-produced piece one buys at a department store for a couple of hundred bucks. If he had known, Kri had no doubt he would've refused to accept it.

Eventually, he would find out. Someone would say something about it and he would go on the Internet to check it out.

Either way, she fully expected him to fight her about it.

Not tonight, though.

CHAPTER 13: MICHAEL

*M*ichael wiped his mouth with a napkin. The meal had been fantastic. Not a big surprise. He'd sampled this restaurant chef's creations before at Kian and Syssi's wedding. While people had been mingling and dancing, Michael had stayed close to the appetizer buffet, stuffing himself with more than his fair share of the small delicacies.

Regrettably though, unlike the spread at the wedding, this hadn't been an all-you-can-eat affair. The three courses had been amazing, but the quantities had been tiny, more a taste than enough to fill up on. He could easily handle a burger or two right now.

Kri was pretending as if she was full, but he knew her capacity wasn't significantly less than his, so she must've been still hungry as well, but he wasn't going to suggest they order more stuff. This outing was probably costing Kri a fortune. She wasn't hurting for money, but he didn't want to feel like a mooch. And this was on top of what she'd already shelled out for the watch, which was at least several hundred.

He took it off his wrist to examine it more closely,

discovering that the underside was made from a clear plastic or some other see-through material, and the watch's intricate mechanism was visible.

"Look at this." He dangled it by the strap so she could see the back. "You can see the thing's guts. It's so cool."

She chuckled. "I know. The salesman at the jewelry store made a big deal out of it."

She bought it at a specialist store? Damn, it must've been more expensive than he thought. "I hope you didn't spend too much on it."

It looked like a simple sports watch, but Michael knew next to nothing about such things. Hell, he didn't even own one. Who needed it when your cellphone could tell you what time it was with perfect accuracy, automatically adjusting for whatever time zone you happened to travel to around the world?

Watches were a thing of the past—a piece of jewelry the older generation still clung to. Which was a reminder that Kri, despite her youthful hotness, had been born a couple of decades before him and hadn't grown up with a smartphone superglued to the palm of her hand.

She smiled. "As long as you like it, it was worth every penny."

He cocked a brow. "It sure doesn't look like something you can buy with a jar of pennies."

Kri shrugged. "So, how did you like dinner? It was delicious, right?"

Clearly, she was trying to change the subject. He should drop it. Inquiring about the price of a gift was rude.

"It was amazing. But it's too pricy and fancy for a regular date, or even for a birthday. A place like this is perfect for a proposal, or celebrating a special anniversary. You know me, I would've been happy with burgers and fries."

Kri crossed her hands over her chest. "It's your birthday, and I wanted to do something special for you."

He took her hand. "I know. Thank you. Next time we come here, though, it will be my treat." He made a point of looking around. "I'm thinking of proposing to you here." He said it with a wink, even though he was a hundred percent serious. Except, Kri would've freaked out, and the wink had been meant to put her at ease.

The snort that left her mouth was somewhat hurtful. "Don't be ridiculous, Michael. Even as a joke it's not funny. You're so young. You haven't experienced life yet. How many women, or rather girls, had you been with before me? One? Two? And you're talking about a lifelong commitment?"

Michael shifted uncomfortably, but didn't reply. Her questions, or rather statements, were offensive and didn't deserve an answer.

Except Kri wasn't very perceptive for a woman, and she completely missed his cues. Either that, or she just wasn't ready to give up. "Joking aside, how many females did you have sex with before me? I'm curious."

Fuck, he really didn't want to answer, but Kri was stubborn, and she'd keep pushing until she got what she wanted.

"One. You're happy now?"

She pouted. "Yes and no. I'm not happy that you have so little to compare me to, but I'm happy that you're mine. Seriously, though, I shouldn't be selfish and keep you for myself. The right thing to do would be to set you free and let you explore. And if you still wanted to come back to me, then great. But I don't know if I could do it. I'd be too jealous."

Damn right, she should be jealous. He couldn't even think of her with another man. What was wrong with her? Was it an immortal thing? Or a Kri thing? Was he the problem? Or was Kri suffering from an acute case of commitment phobia?

Michael shook his head. "What am I to you, Kri? A

boyfriend? A friend with benefits? A boy toy? How can you even think about me with someone else?" He threw his napkin on the table and got up. "I need some fresh air. I'll wait for you by the front door." Michael was boiling inside, and it had taken a lot of self-discipline to temper his response to something that sounded semi-civil.

What he really wanted to do was march back to the parking lot, get in the car, and drive off.

Somewhere in the back of his mind, Michael was aware that he was overreacting. Kri might've lacked tact and had spoken without thinking, but she had taken it back just as soon as she'd blurted it out. Letting him fool around with someone else was just as abhorrent to her as it was to him. Or at least he hoped so.

Problem was, it was quite obvious that he loved her more than she loved him.

If she loved him at all.

Kri never said the words. Neither had he, but only because he was afraid of her reaction.

Perhaps it was time to stop being a chicken and lay it all out on the table. The truth was that Kri had stolen his heart right from the start, and when she'd taken him in after his transition they had become an item. But they had never discussed the future, and Michael had no idea where he stood with her.

Not that he was in any position to make demands when he had nothing to offer. Before the big talk he was planning on having with Kri, he'd hoped to make some headway with the Guardian training first—to get to be at least good enough to start receiving a trainee salary.

Arwel had explained that Guardians trained for decades before earning the title, and as a full-time commitment was required, no one expected them to be doing it for free. Once a certain threshold was met, and a person was officially accepted as a Guardian in training, he or she started getting paid. It was less than half of what the Guardians were making, but it was good pay nonetheless.

When declaring his love and asking Kri to make a commitment to him, he shouldn't be the guy who lived on an allowance and didn't have a job or even a prospect of one.

How would she ever take him seriously?

Trouble was, Michael now knew that he still had a lot of training ahead of him before he got officially accepted into the program, and telling Kri how he felt couldn't wait that long.

He'd almost blown it with her by working himself into exhaustion while trying to hasten his acceptance. It had taken his thick skull too long to realize what she must have been thinking. It seemed that Kri had gotten it into her head that he was training so hard because she'd done better than him in that alley fight.

Silly girl.

This wasn't about some stupid competition, or worse, about her being a female with superior fighting skills to his meager ones. How could she ever think that? Was her opinion of him so low?

Hell, he was damn proud of Kri and her awe-inspiring performance.

What had really happened that night was that he'd realized how far he still had to go.

No one had told him that it would take him decades to become a fully-fledged Guardian, or that all his work up till now had been just training to get accepted into the program. Before telling Kri that he loved her and wished to spend the rest of his immortal life with her, Michael had wanted to have at least this one thing accomplished. Except, it seemed that he needed to revise his plan.

CHAPTER 14: KRI

*W*ith a heavy sigh, Kri finished telling Amanda and Syssi about the mess last night had turned out to be. Instead of making things better between Michael and her, she'd managed to make them worse.

"You didn't…" Amanda gasped.

Kri grimaced. She'd bungled things pretty bad with Michael. What had possessed her to suggest he needed to experience sex with other females? Sometimes her big mouth talked before her brain had time to weigh the consequences.

Fuck.

Everything had been going so well, he'd seemed so happy, and then she'd put that hurt expression on his handsome face. She was such an idiot.

"Yeah, I did. And I don't know how to fix it. We've been making such good progress and then I had to shoot off my stupid mouth."

Grabbing the end tail of her braid, Kri twisted it between her fingers. "It's just that he startled me with all this talk about proposing. He just turned twenty-one for Fates' sake, and he is talking about marriage? A lifelong commitment? I felt like I needed to throw some cold water on his head to cool him down."

"I think it's sweet that he is so serious about you." Syssi handed Kri a cup of cappuccino and sat across from Amanda and her.

After the By Invitation Only fiasco, Kri had called an emergency meeting with the girls, and it had been decided to hold it at Syssi's place. Kian was working late that night, so they had their privacy without having to kick anyone out of his home. Kri still felt bad about chasing Dalhu out of his own living room the other night.

"It's stupid, that's what it is. He is just a kid. Hell, I still feel like a kid. I'm not ready to make such a serious commitment."

Syssi lifted a brow. "Do you love him?"

"I do, but that doesn't mean I want to marry him. Someday, maybe, but not in the near future, that's for sure."

The corners of Syssi's lips lifted in the kind of smile that suggested she knew things Kri didn't.

Well, duh, Syssi was a married woman.

True, in years she was nearly half Kri's age, but Syssi had been a human up until recently. Prior to her lifetime horizon expanding indefinitely, she'd been forced to develop a more mature attitude. At twenty-five, a quarter of her allotted time had been used up. And that had been a best case scenario, provided that she lived into old age and didn't die sooner of some disease.

"Maybe all he needs is to be reassured that you're serious about him," Amanda said.

Yeah, like she didn't know that.

But there were several reasons she hadn't told Michael she loved him yet. First of all, they had been together only a couple of months. Second, he was already becoming a permanent fixture in her life, and it was scaring the crap out of her. Third, even without any declarations of love, the boy was talking marriage, for Fates' sake. The last thing she wanted was to encourage him.

"That's the thing, though, I'm not sure that I am serious about him. I think I'm too young to make decisions that will affect the rest of my life. Falling for the first available immortal male who is not related to me is such a cliché. You know what I mean?" Kri pushed to her feet and began pacing.

"Hey, I fell for the first immortal male I was not related to." Amanda crossed her arms over her chest.

Syssi raised a finger. "Not true. You met Andrew first, and you knew that he was a Dormant—a potential immortal. In fact, before Dalhu kidnapped you, I suspected there was something going on between you and Andrew. Not that I don't think Dalhu is perfect for you, but for a while there I entertained hope that you and Andrew might end up together."

"Well, that's even worse, isn't it?" Amanda waved her hand at Kri. "You want to talk about cliché? I fell in love with my kidnapper."

Kri stopped to glare at Amanda. "The fact that you fell for Dalhu proves nothing. I'm not saying that you made the wrong decision to commit to him, but at the time you hadn't thought it through. You were acting on pure impulse like you always do."

"Pfft, you don't know what you're talking about. I agonized for days, trying to convince myself that I could live without him. Dalhu was the last male on earth I wanted to be bound to for life. But when the Fates decide who is the one for you, you can fight it as much as you want, but you'll only make yourself miserable. Trust me, been there, done that."

Ugh, Fates this and Fates that. Amanda was supposed to be a scientist, not someone who believed in divine intervention.

"So what are you saying? That the Fates decide everything and we have no say in it? And how do you know it is really fate? And not your overactive hormones that are guiding your decision? Eh?"

"Come on, girls, this is not a constructive conversation." Syssi shushed them both. "What Amanda is trying to say is that falling in love is not rational. It is a gut feeling and it often happens pretty fast. Subconsciously, we know it right away. I'll never forget my reaction to Kian. From the first moment, I knew I wanted him more than I'd wanted anyone or anything in my life before, but I thought he was out of my league. Rationally, I tried to convince myself that a man like him could never want someone like me. I fought so hard not to fall in love with him, to regard it as a sexual fling, believing I'd only get hurt if I allowed myself to feel. And he fought it too. A mortal and an immortal had no future together. But it was all futile. We fell head over heels in love with each other even though we both believed our relationship was doomed."

On an exhale, Kri plopped back onto the couch and dropped her head on the overstuffed pillows. It seemed that a rocky start was a norm and not the exception in a relationship. Syssi and Kian were so in love with each other it was impossible not to be a little jealous of that. And so were Amanda and Dalhu. But it hadn't been smooth sailing for either of the couples.

Kri had some soul searching to do.

Was Michael her fated one?

Was her gut telling her that he was, but she was too chicken to acknowledge it?

How would she know for sure?

"I get what you're trying to say. Problem is, I don't know

what my gut is telling me. How do I listen to something I can't hear?"

Amanda and Syssi exchanged looks, but it was Amanda who answered Kri's question. "I guess that for some it's easier than others. I ran away to get some distance between me and Dalhu, but I missed him and craved him terribly. Every day that passed was worse than the one before it. In the end, I was forced to accept the truth. My life with Dalhu was going to be difficult. There were so many obstacles on the way, some that at the time seemed insurmountable, but on the other hand, I realized that life without him was going to be hell. Perhaps I should've had more faith in fate—and in Dalhu. He was willing to do whatever it took to be with me, and he did. Sweet merciful Fates, how he did." Amanda shuddered.

Dalhu was a remarkable male, no doubt about it. Kri had witnessed herself what he'd gone through to be with Amanda and become part of her world.

To redeem himself in the eyes of the clan as well as Amanda's, Dalhu had submitted to a trial that would've felled the vast majority of men. Standing tall, unaided and unrestrained, he'd withstood a whipping that had stripped most of the skin off his back. After that, he'd been entombed for a whole week, which meant that he'd been practically dead for seven days before being revived.

That night, witnessing his incredible sacrifice, Kri had stopped regarding Dalhu as a Doomer, or even an ex-Doomer. In her eyes, and probably in the eyes of all who'd witnessed it, he'd become the brave male who had gone through hell and back for the woman he loved. He'd been forgiven and accepted into the clan. Something no one would've ever dreamed possible.

Dalhu was the best example of love-conquers-all.

Would Michael go to such extremes for her?

Kri shuddered. She'd rather go through hell herself than let him suffer. After all, Michael was just a kid.

Was he, though?

CHAPTER 15: MICHAEL

*M*ichael staggered as Arwel's punch got through his defenses. Once again.

"Pay attention, kid. You're not focused today."

It was true. The turmoil in his head was too loud for the soft whisper of his telepathy to penetrate through it.

"I know. I'm trying," he said.

Arwel shook his head. "Let's take a break. You're worse now than you were at the beginning of our training. You're not only unfocused, but you're angry and aggressive instead of cool and collected like you should be. You need to tell me what's going on with you."

Michael put his hands on his hips and dropped his head. Even with his extraordinary telepathic ability, Arwel wouldn't understand. These immortals screwed around with numerous partners and thought nothing of it. Kri's suggestion that he should sample more females before settling down with her would seem perfectly logical to the guy.

"By the waves of anger you're emitting, I'm guessing it's a woman problem. Did Kri and you have a spat?"

"It wasn't a fight. She said something that I found insulting, that's all. I know she didn't mean to offend me. But what she said made me realize that she couldn't be possibly serious about me."

Arwel frowned. "She loves you. That is obvious. Why would you think she is not serious?"

"Does she?" She'd never told him. But if Arwel felt it, then perhaps she really did.

"Of course she does. Every time I see you with Kri, I get nauseated from all the mushy sentiment she radiates. You too, by the way. It's totally disgusting. She's also incredibly proud of you, and that's disgusting too." Arwel was smiling throughout his insults, perhaps because Michael's expression was morphing from a frustrated scowl into a silly, face-splitting grin.

Kri loved him? And she was proud of him? Why?

"I don't understand. There is nothing to be proud of. I've accomplished nothing, I have nothing to offer her. I live at her apartment without sharing in the expenses, whatever they may be. And my monthly income is an allowance Kian is giving me because he is a generous guy, not because I merit it in any way."

Arwel was nodding as if he was agreeing with everything Michael was saying. Couldn't the guy at least pretend it wasn't true? Be supportive?

"I understand your problem, kid, and it has nothing to do with what Kri feels or doesn't feel for you. This is about your own self-perception, and the story you tell yourself. If you think you're worthless, then you expect everyone to think the same. If you believe you're a mooch, then everyone else must believe it too. But guess what?"

"What?"

"They don't. What I, and Kri, and Kian, and everyone else sees, is a young man who works his butt off to prove himself. A man who knows what he wants and goes for it with all he has. And that includes the woman he loves. You're very grown up for your age."

That was certainly a good thing to hear, and even with his dim telepathic ability, Michael felt that Arwel had meant everything he'd said.

The guy wasn't done, though. "You already have a clear vision for your future, which is astounding at your age. Compared to you, I'm ancient, and the only sure thing in my life is being a Guardian. Everything else is a disgusting mess."

It seemed that Arwel was repulsed by a lot of things.

"Thank you for the pep talk, but if what you are saying is true, and Kri shares your opinion, then why have I never heard any of it from her? She's never even told me that she loves me."

Arwel lifted a brow. "Did you tell her you loved her?"

"Well, no. She gets so defensive anytime I mention anything about commitment that I turn it into a joke so she doesn't bolt like her tail is on fire. I'm afraid that if I tell her I love her she'll freak out."

Arwel stared at him for a moment, and then he walked over to where he'd left his phone next to the wall, lifted the thing off the floor, and started texting.

"What are you doing?" Michael asked, even though he had a sinking feeling he knew who the message was going to.

"I'm telling your girlfriend to get her ass in here, so you can tell her how you feel about her."

As panic gripped his heart and squeezed, Michael imagined doing the same to Arwel's neck. "You are a fucking asshole, you know that? What I've told you wasn't for sharing, especially not with Kri."

Arwel lifted his hand, palm out. "Relax, kid. I just told her you need a sparring partner for this session and asked if she was free. I told her nothing about your mushy feelings. I leave that up to you."

"Phew, you almost gave me a stroke, if I were still human, that is." Michael slapped a hand over his heart. It was beating so hard against his ribcage that he could feel it all the way through the slabs of muscle covering his chest. The thing was hammering against his palm as if it wanted to get out.

"Well, then you're lucky that you're no longer a mortal. It's a mixed blessing, though. It will take so much longer for to you pass out from the beating I'll give you for calling me a fucking asshole." The smile on Arwel's face was not friendly. In fact, the guy looked scary.

Was he really that pissed?

Michael closed his eyes and focused his senses.

Nah. Arwel had been messing with him. The guy wasn't angry. He was amused… and hungry.

Michael walked over to his mentor and offered his hand. "I'm sorry. It was uncalled for. Thank you for being chill about it."

Arwel grinned as he gripped Michael's hand, squeezing it tight and pulling him in for a clap on the back and a brief embrace. "You're welcome, kid. Just don't let it happen again. Part of becoming a warrior is learning to keep your cool or at least faking it really well."

"I will."

"Tell Kri hi from me when she gets here."

"What, you're not going to stay?"

Arwel rubbed his stomach. "Nope. I'm going to grab something to eat. You can handle this." Lifting his gym bag, Arwel paused before heading out the door. "Courage, kid. At least one of you needs to be brave enough to say what needs saying."

Ain't that the truth.

CHAPTER 16: KRI

Interesting. Kri frowned as she read the text message. It had arrived a few minutes ago, but she didn't see it until after her workout was done and she'd picked up her things to go home.

Michael needed a sparring partner?

Why her, though?

The last thing she wanted was to make things worse between them by beating the shit out of her boyfriend.

She couldn't lose even if she wanted to, and she didn't want to.

It would be the same as lying.

She was not going to hold back just because Michael had a fragile ego. The best thing was to refuse. Let Arwel rope in another Guardian to do the honors. Michael wouldn't feel as bad getting beat up by one of the guys.

Her fingers flew over the phone's keyboard. *Not a good idea. Find someone else.* She sent the text, grabbed her towel, and waved goodbye to Bhathian.

A second later, her phone pinged. *Get your butt in here. He needs your help to practice evasive moves.*

Damn.

Perhaps Arwel was meaning to use her just to demonstrate. If he asked her to spar with Michael, she could always refuse. Arwel wasn't her commander, and they were not on a mission where she had to cooperate. Unless Onegus issued an order, Kri was under no obligation to do as her fellow Guardian asked.

Despite his seniority, their status in the force was equal.

With a curse, she turned away from the bank of elevators and headed down the hallway to the classroom Arwel's text had directed her to.

When she entered, Kri found Michael alone in the room. "Where is Arwel?"

"Not here." Michael looked uncomfortable.

"I can see that. I thought he wanted to demonstrate evasive moves on me." Heck, maybe Michael would jump on the opportunity to cop out. "Is he coming back?"

"He said he was going to get something to eat, but he didn't say anything about returning." Michael rubbed a hand over his neck. "I've been practicing using telepathy to anticipate my opponent's moves. I can try and show you what I've learned. Problem is, I can't read you. You're either blocking me, or I'm blocking myself. So it might not work."

Eh, what the hell. She could go a round or two with him.

No more, though.

"Let's give it a try. Nothing fancy, just some basic moves to see if you can sense me coming at you. Okay?"

"That's the idea."

"I'm not going to hold back."

He looked puzzled. "Why the hell would you? I won't break. As Arwel has proven time and again, I can take a lot of abuse. I swear, the guy enjoys hurting me."

Hmm. Michael seemed to take his defeat for granted, and it didn't look as if the prospect troubled him. On the contrary, he didn't like the idea of her going easy on him because she didn't want to hurt him.

Had she been wrong?

Perhaps it wasn't about her being a girl who was a better fighter than him.

But if that wasn't it, then what was his problem?

Kri dropped her towel on the floor and put her phone on top of it.

Returning to the mat, she assumed the opening stance. "Are you ready?"

Michael mirrored her pose—knees slightly bent, his balance centered on his core muscles. Kri feinted to the right, then punched with her left. Her fist connected with his middle and Michael was thrown back a couple of feet.

"God, you're strong," he wheezed. "And fast. I knew you were going to do that, but I didn't dodge in time."

"That's why we train so long and so hard. If you have to think you're already too late. Your response has to be automatic, a reflex, and that only comes with endless repetition."

"I get it. Let's try again."

"Are you sure? You're not ready for full contact yet. You should practice with a protective suit."

"Nah, I'd rather hurt all over than wear that stinky, sweaty thing. Besides, I heal so fast that it's really not a problem."

If she went at him full force, this was going to be brutal, and unnecessary. Except, any less than her best would offend him.

Two more moves and that was it.

"Ready?"

He gave her a nod.

Lunging at Michael as if intending to tackle him, Kri changed trajectory at the last moment and delivered a roundhouse kick. This time he was faster, and her foot only connected with the tip of his ear. Which could have hurt like a son-of-a-bitch if she were wearing boots. But a brush of her toes wasn't so bad.

"This was good, Michael. Did you anticipate my move?"

Holding his palm over his ear, Michael grinned. "Yeah, I did. Instead of trying to guess it, I let instinct guide me. And it worked! I'm amazed."

"That's exactly what you need to do. You have the instincts of a good fighter. Now let me kiss the hurt away." She sauntered up to him and pulled away his hand, then very gently kissed his red and swollen ear.

"Hmm, that feels nice." Michael wrapped his arm around her and brought her flush against him. "And this is even better." His palm clamped over her nape, holding her in place as he turned to kiss her.

Kri's lips parted in invitation, which he accepted with a leisurely sweep of his tongue. They were both sweaty from their workouts, but Kri couldn't care less. She wanted to get Michael naked right there on the rubber training mat.

"I want you," she breathed into his mouth.

"Here?"

"Yes."

"Naughty girl. What if Arwel comes back?"

Kri smirked. "I'm going to make so much noise that anyone passing by this door will know not to come in."

"Oh yeah? What kind of noise?" He trailed his lips down her neck then bit down where it met her shoulder.

With a groan, Kri's eyelids dropped over her eyes, and she tilted her head sideways to give him better access.

"Oh, this kind of noise." Michael licked the little hurt away then bit down on a different spot.

Fates, she loved when he did that—couldn't wait for his fangs to grow fully and deliver the aphrodisiac she craved to experience.

Michael tensed as her hand reached between their bodies and snaked into his loose exercise pants. She gripped his hard length, rubbing her thumb over the moist head. His big body shuddered and he pushed up into her palm.

For a moment, he only held her close as she pleasured him, her hand stroking his length and spreading his own lubrication all over it.

Damn, her gym shorts were getting soaking wet, and she needed Michael to do something about it before she exploded.

As if reading her mind, he shoved the stretchy shorts down her legs and put two fingers inside her.

"Fates, yes. Oh, yes…" she moaned as he began thrusting those thick digits in and out of her. Except, as good as this was, she wanted something other than his fingers inside her. With a strong tug, she had his pants and his boxer shorts drop down to his ankles.

He kicked them off then pulled his muscle shirt over his head and tossed it down to the mat. Gloriously nude, he unhooked her sport bra and helped her get rid of it.

As soon as Kri divested herself of the rest, Michael grabbed her ass and hoisted her up. She wrapped her legs around his hips and her arms around his neck, kissing him hard as he carried her to the nearest wall.

Holding her up with one hand, he guided his shaft inside her sheath, filling her with one hard thrust. She almost climaxed right there, and if he had moved, she probably would. Except, Michael knew her body so well, read every nuance so readily, that he remained still inside her, waiting for the pulsing waves to subside. It was too soon for her.

Naturally, she could climax again and again, but none were as powerful as the first one.

When she opened her eyes, Kri expected Michael's expression to be pained. It wasn't easy to hold still while every fiber in his body was urging him to move. Instead, what she saw was love.

His young face was so handsome, so honest and sincere, so open. Even though he'd never verbalized his feelings for her, he wasn't afraid to show them. Who needed talking when his attitude and his deeds spoke much louder than any words ever could?

Kri put her hands on his cheeks and looked into his eyes as she told him, "I love you, Michael."

CHAPTER 17: MICHAEL

*I*f Kri hadn't been looking straight into his eyes as she said she loved him, Michael would've thought he'd imagined it. He'd waited so long to hear her say it that it might as well have been a hallucination. Except, from a distance of less than a few inches, there could've been no mistake.

For a moment, he froze, nothing other than panting breaths coming out of his mouth, but then Kri smiled and said it for him. "Take a breath and say, I love you too, Kri."

Like an idiot, he nodded.

Come on, man, say something!

He cleared his throat. "I love you, Kri, so much. You're the most beautiful, amazing woman there is. You're one of a kind —the one and only for me."

A single tear slid down her cheek. "This is the nicest thing anyone has ever said to me."

Michael wiped the tear away.

Even though this was exactly what Arwel had in mind, it had been so unexpected. Up against the wall, in a classroom converted into a training area, was not where Michael had imagined telling Kri he loved her, but it was perfect nonetheless.

His woman wasn't big on romance.

Which she proved when she smiled evilly and said, "Baby, I love you, but if you don't start moving soon, I'm going to punch you in the nose."

Yep, definitely not a romantic. But one hell of a dynamo in bed, or against the wall, or on the kitchen counter…

Did he forget something?

Oh, yeah. In the back seat of her Hummer, and in a club against the bathroom's counter. As he was reminded of their adventures, Michael gripped Kri's ass and plowed into her. "Remember the time in the club?" he whispered in her ear.

"Aha…" she moaned her answer.

"In the bathroom?"

"Yeah?"

"We didn't sample the one in By Invitation Only. Next time, I'm going to fuck you there."

Kri managed another, "Ahaaaa…"

"You'd like it, wouldn't you?"

"Ahaaaa…"

Their version of dirty talk was pushing all the right buttons for Kri. The more he talked, the wilder she got, meeting every thrust with a forceful one of her own until he wasn't sure who was fucking whom.

"I'm going to make you scream so loud, everyone is going to hear you. They are going to call the cops on us."

Kri groaned, her head hitting the wall.

She was close, and so was he. Talking was becoming difficult. They were going at each other with such force that the plaster was cracking all over where he had Kri pressed against the wall. Michael had the passing thought that it was good the thing was built from blocks and not drywall. They would've punched right through it.

With the pressure reaching the point of no return, Michael felt his fangs pulsate even though his venom glands were still inert, and he struck Kri's neck, biting down at the same time as his seed shot into her. She exploded, her inner muscles milking his shaft until there was nothing left.

"Let's continue upstairs?" he said once he caught his breath.

Sweaty, messy, and smelling of sex, they left the class-room giggling like a couple of idiots and dashed for the elevators. Thankfully, no one hitched a ride with them, and they made it back to their place with no one the wiser.

After another round in the shower, they finally made it to the bed for the third one. This was the one Michael liked the best. The first and the second were about the needs of the flesh. The last one was about closeness, togetherness. It was about love.

"I love you, baby," he said as they lay facing each other, their limbs entwined, spent and satiated.

Kri chuckled. "I love you too. I don't know why it took me so long to tell you that I do. I knew I loved you from almost day one."

"Me too. Remember when I asked you if you were married?"

"Yes, and I replied that it was none of your business."

"Well, it was. I knew that I had found the one woman who was perfect for me, and I was willing to go to war for you."

"You were? It's so sweet."

"Still am. Even if the one I have to fight is you."

Kri lifted her eyes. "Me? What do you have to fight me for?"

"Us. This is not a fling for me, Kri. I'm not thinking about sampling other females, as you suggested. As far as I'm concerned, I'm done looking. I've found my one and only."

She cast him a sheepish glance. "About that. I don't know why I said it. Sometimes my mouth blurts nonsense before my brain tells it what it should and shouldn't say. I didn't mean it. Hell, I'd probably beat up any female that tried to put her hooks in you. You're mine."

"Does it mean that you'll no longer freak out and run for the hills when I mention commitment? Marriage?"

She shifted in his arms, and for a moment Michael thought that he'd pushed her too far.

"It's not that I don't want to commit to you, or that I don't see us getting officially mated one day. It's just that we are still young. I'm not saying no, I'm saying not yet."

"Then when? All I want is a commitment. I'm not asking you to marry me tomorrow, although I would, in a heartbeat, but I want to hear you say that you will at some definite time in the future. Vague promises are meaningless."

Kri kissed his chin and hugged him closer. "I'll tell you what. You go back to college and get your bachelor's degree first. If you still want to marry me after that, we have a date."

Sneaky woman.

"Fine, but I have some conditions of my own."

"Let's hear them."

"I don't have time for regular classes. I still want to dedicate most of my energy to training. But I can enroll in an online university and study in the evenings."

"I'm okay with that."

"That's not all. You enroll with me. We can study together and get our diplomas at the same time."

Kri didn't answer right away, her beautiful face changing expressions as she thought it over. He didn't need telepathy to figure out what she was thinking.

"I guess it's only fair. I can't ask you to do something I'm not willing to do. Besides, it will be fun. Are you going to tutor me if I need it? It has been a while since I graduated high school."

"Sure, if you pay me."

She narrowed her eyes. "What type of payment do you have in mind?"

Michael pressed his hardening erection into her belly. "The best kind."

Kri grinned. "I have to warn you, baby. I'm going to need lots and lots of tutoring."

The End.

READY FOR ANDREW'S STORY?
BOOK 7: DARK WARRIOR MINE

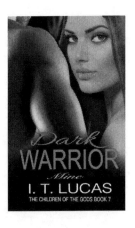

READ THE ENCLOSED EXCERPT

DEAR READER,

Thank you for reading the ***Children of the Gods***. If you enjoyed the story, I would be grateful if you could leave a short review on Amazon.

With a few words, you'll make me very happy. (-:

Click here to leave a review

Love & happy reading,
Isabell

BOOK 7: DARK WARRIOR MINE

When Andrew is forced to retire from active duty, he believes that a boring desk job is all he has to look forward to. His glory days in special ops are over. But as it turns out, his thrill ride has just begun. Andrew discovers not only that immortals exist and have been manipulating global affairs since antiquity, but that he and his sister are rare possessors of the immortal genes.

Problem is, Andrew might be too old to attempt the activation process. His sister, who is fourteen years his junior, barely makes it through the transition, so the odds of him coming out of it alive, let alone immortal, are slim.

But fate may force his hand.

EXCERPT

Harvard-Westlake High school
Studio City, California
13 years ago.

"Hi, Nathalie." Leaning his hip against the metal door of his locker, Luke Bruoker produced his seductive smile. For her.

Walk away, the voice in her head commanded.

Shut up, Nathalie thought back.

Just do it. You know what he's thinking.

As if she needed Tut to freaking tell her what was on Luke's mind as he flashed her, *Nutty Nattie,* the perfect set of teeth that had all the other girls wetting their designer panties. With his good looks and rich daddy, Luke was one of the most popular guys in school, and for giving her the time of day, he probably expected her to fall at his feet in gratitude.

Not this girl, not going to happen, buddy.

Trying to ignore her too handsome and too full of himself locker neighbor, Nathalie stuffed the books she came to retrieve in her backpack.

But what if she was wrong? What if Luke was just being nice? And anyway, even if he wasn't, she didn't want to be rude.

"Hi, Luke." Nathalie lifted the corners of her lips in a tight smile and waved goodbye.

You're not wrong, Tut snickered. *But if it's any consolation, he thinks you're hot.*

It's not.

Unfortunately, there was no way to hide things from the stowaway sharing her cranium space.

You're such a liar. Tut's laugh echoed in her head before slowly fading away.

Well, what did he expect? She was only human and couldn't help but feel flattered.

He was such a pain, but if she was lucky, for the next few hours he'd leave her alone. Tut, or *tutor*, as he'd introduced himself after chasing all the other voices away, hated math class. In fact, the ghost in her head didn't like school, or homework, or tests—which was probably the main reason she was such a good student. The only time Nathalie could be alone in her own skull was while studying.

Tut claimed to be teaching her about life.

Yeah, right, more like ruining it.

Watching TV with him was a nightmare. He wouldn't shut up for a moment with his nonstop derisive commentary about everyone and everything. And hanging out with friends or going to the mall was more of the same.

Who was she kidding? As if anyone wanted to hang out with Nutty Nattie—the girl who talked to herself.

Nathalie pulled on the straps of her heavy backpack,

hitching it higher on her back as she walked faster—pretending to rush so no one would notice that she always walked alone.

Mostly, she felt invisible. No one would look at her, except maybe for some of the nicer girls who would occasionally give her a pitying smile—as if she was retarded or deformed. The best she could hope for was to be regarded as the crazy genius. Unfortunately, even though she was smart and worked harder than most, she deserved only the first part of the title.

But at least her hard work had gotten her accepted into this overpriced private high school. Trouble was, her parents couldn't really afford it—not even with the generous financial aid they'd been awarded—and she knew for a fact that they were dipping into their equity line to finance the difference. The school called the discount a scholarship, but it wasn't. None of the rich kids were getting it, not even those who were excellent students.

Still, it wasn't as if anyone was privy to that information, but it wasn't hard to guess either. Her classmates arrived at school in Mercedes and BMWs while she drove a three-year-old Toyota Corolla hatchback.

Not that she was complaining, her car was great—the previous owner had hardly driven her, and she was almost as good as new. Besides, this was the best her parents could afford. God knew they had always given her everything they could, and probably more than they should—spoiling their only child.

When she was younger, she'd thought it was her due, but lately, it was making her feel guilty. It seemed as if by giving her all of their love, her parents were left with nothing for each other.

In fact, this morning, her mother told her that she'd filed for a divorce.

Oh, God, what is Papi going to do?

The coffee shop wasn't making much, and they would not have been able to afford much of anything without her mother's government pension.

How is Papi going to survive without it?

Thank God, it was her last year of high school, so at least this expense would be gone. And since she'd gotten a full-ride scholarship to the University of Virginia, college wouldn't cost her parents anything.

But savings aside, it meant that her father would be all alone once she left.

At sixty, her mother was still a knockout, while Papi, two years her junior, looked like a grandpa. It had to do with his love of baking—and eating. He was at least fifty pounds overweight and almost bald. But he was the sweetest guy. Which was probably why his business wasn't doing so well. He had never turned away anyone who was hungry, regardless of their ability to pay.

Not fair.

The God her father believed in so earnestly should've smiled upon a man like him, rewarded him for his good heart and generosity. But instead, his beloved coffee shop was barely staying afloat, and his beautiful wife was leaving him.

Nathalie had a feeling that her mother had just been waiting for her to finish school and go to college to make her move. Eva hadn't been happy for years—even when Papi had been much thinner and still had hair. She always looked troubled, almost fearful, though Nathalie couldn't figure out why.

Maybe her mother suffered from some mental disease— like Nathalie did. Though instead of hearing voices of dead people in her head, Eva might've been anxious or depressed.

It was about time she talked with her mother and cleared things up. She was definitely old enough for a grownup conversation. Perhaps they both could benefit from psychiatric help. And maybe, just maybe, with treatment, Eva might change her mind about leaving.

But even if she wouldn't, to be rid of Tut, it was worth a try.

Problem was, psychiatrists were expensive.

Maybe that was why her parents had never taken her to one, even though they must've known that her so-called imaginary friends had been very different than those of other kids.

But Papi had said that it was harmless, nothing to worry about, and her mother had agreed. They'd cautioned her that it was okay to play pretend at home, but she shouldn't be talking to herself in public.

Nathalie had tried.

As she had grown older, she'd realized that it wasn't normal and that the people talking to her in her head were probably just elaborate hallucinations. A mental disorder and not ghosts. She'd stopped telling even her parents about it.

But here and there, she would forget herself and respond out loud—hence the damn nickname. *Nutty Nattie*.

DARK WARRIOR MINE
Is Available on Amazon

SERIES READING ORDER

TRY THE SERIES ON

AUDIBLE

2 FREE audiobooks with your new Audible subscription!

FOR EXCLUSIVE PEEKS
Join The Children Of The Gods VIP Club
and gain access to the VIP portal at ITLUCAS.COM
click here to join

Included in your free membership:

- **FREE** narration of Goddess's Choice—Book 1 in The Children of the Gods Origins series.
- Preview chapters.
- And other exclusive content offered only to my VIPs.

43704063R00071

Made in the USA
Lexington, KY
01 July 2019